LIKE ABILITY

⩶ THE TRUTH ABOUT POPULARITY ⩶

*To Brian, Charlie, and Lainey, who inspire me daily to be
the best person I can be. And when I don't get it right,
remind me that I get to try again tomorrow—LG*

*To Samara, Max, and my wife, Tina, who teach me every
day about the relationships that matter most—MP*

Books for Kids From the
American Psychological Association
maginationpress.org

Copyright © 2022 by Magination Press, an imprint of the American Psychological
Association. All rights reserved. Except as permitted under the United States
Copyright Act of 1976, no part of this publication may be reproduced or distributed
in any form or by any means, or stored in a database or retrieval system, without the
prior written permission of the publisher.

Magination Press is a registered trademark of the American Psychological
Association. Order books at maginationpress.org or call 1-800-374-2721.

Book design by Rachel Ross
Printed by Sheridan, Chelsea, MI

Library of Congress Cataloging-in-Publication Data
Names: Getz, Lori, author. | Prinstein, Mitchell J., 1970- author.
Title: Like ability: the truth about popularity/Lori Getz, MA & Mitch Prinstein, Ph.D.
Other titles: Likeability
Description: [Washington]: Magination Press, [2022] | Audience: Ages 11-14 |
Audience: Grades 7-9 | Summary: "A workbook for teens about what popularity
is, why some kinds are healthier than others, and how teens can grow their social
intelligence"—Provided by publisher.
Identifiers: LCCN 2021039758 (print) | LCCN 2021039759 (ebook) | ISBN
9781433833632 (hardcover) | ISBN 9781433838408 (ebook)
Subjects: LCSH: Social interaction—Juvenile literature. | Popularity—Juvenile
literature. | Social intelligence—Juvenile literature. | BISAC: YOUNG ADULT
NONFICTION/Social Topics/Friendship | YOUNG ADULT NONFICTION/Social
Topics/Self-Esteem & Self-Reliance
Classification: LCC HM1111.G48 2022 (print) | LCC HM1111 (ebook) | DDC 302.1—
dc23/eng/20211025
LC record available at https://lccn.loc.gov/2021039758
LC ebook record available at https://lccn.loc.gov/2021039759

Manufactured in the United States of America
10 9 8 7 6 5 4 3 2 1

LIKE ABILITY

≋ THE TRUTH ABOUT POPULARITY ≋

LORI GETZ, MA, &
MITCH PRINSTEIN, PHD, ABPP

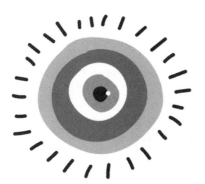

MAGINATION PRESS · WASHINGTON, DC · AMERICAN PSYCHOLOGICAL ASSOCIATION

TABLE OF CONTENTS

Introduction   vii

Section 1: Popularity: What Is It?

Chapter 1: Defining Popularity   3

Chapter 2: What Is Likability?   9

Chapter 3: What Is Status?   29

SECTION 2: Why Do We Want It?

Chapter 4: The Science Behind Popularity   43

Chapter 5: Status Within Status   55

SECTION 3: How Did THEY Get It?

Chapter 6: How Celebrities Find Popularity   65

Chapter 7: The Role of Influencers   73

Chapter 8: Power and Status   87

SECTION 4: Why Is It So Complicated?

Chapter 9: Cue Interpretation   105

Chapter 10: Self-Esteem vs. Peer-Esteem   117

Chapter 11: Complicated Relationships   131

SECTION 5: How Do We Get It?

Chapter 12: How to Be Likable   147

Chapter 13: Emotional Intelligence   157

Chapter 14: Avoiding Temptation to Seek Status   165

Chapter 15: Making a Plan   175

Chapter 16: Managing Expectations   183

Conclusion   193
Glossary   195
About the Authors   198

INTRODUCTION

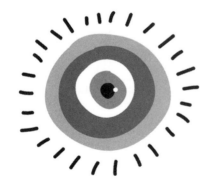

If we asked you what you care about, what would be on the list? Probably some standard answers like school, family, and being a good person—but what else? We've often found that when people are being honest, they spend a lot of time thinking about what others think of them and about their relationships with peers. Who is friends with whom? Who is most popular? What are classmates posting on social media? Social dynamics have always been complicated, even when previous generations were growing up without the internet, but things are far more complex today. Now, teens live in a fishbowl where every action and relationship can be subject to comments, approval, and even ratings. It's a new world that most adults have a hard time relating to and understanding.

Parents try (mostly without success) to explain teen culture to teens. They do their best to sort through the drama, desperately trying to keep up with all the players and their relationships. They mean well. They are wise (due to the many years they too spent as teens). But no matter how smart a parent might be, you probably don't want to hear, "When I was your age..."

So instead, we (the authors) decided it was time to write about popularity for YOU rather than for your parents. This workbook is NOT about knocking down those who are popular, or an attempt to convince you that popularity is a bad thing. In fact, all the research points to the exact opposite: popularity is important!

Instead, we offer you something different: science and research, stories, and an opportunity to decide for yourself which type of popularity YOU want to have. Popularity is not an elusive goal granted only to a select few. Believe it or not, anyone can become the right kind of popular with a little bit of insight and a whole lot of reflection.

This workbook is filled with stories that will make you wonder, shake your head, laugh, and most of all, think about yourself.

We want to give you the information without the lectures! We want you to find yourself in the stories so you can identify who you are right now and who you want to be.

First, we'll talk about what popularity is, and what the different types are. Then we'll talk about why popularity is important—what makes people care about it in the first place? We'll look at how people get popularity, why it's so complicated, and finally, how you can affect your own popularity. Each chapter has activities and prompts to help you reflect on the concepts and create an understanding of how to approach different situations. The goal of the workbook is to encourage and promote self-awareness and develop your individual recipe for the right kind of popular. So are you in? Are you ready to learn the truth about popularity, why it's important, and how to achieve the kind you want? If so, here we go!

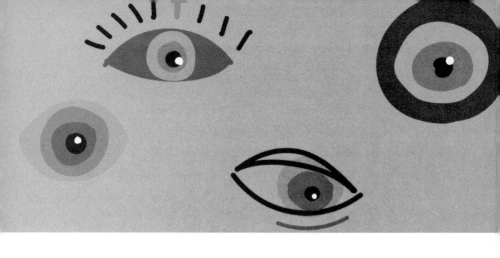

SECTION I

POPULARITY: WHAT IS IT?

Pretty much everyone thinks, has thought, or will think about popularity at some point, whether they're popular or not. They talk about who's popular, wonder about their own standing, and maybe even spend hours online clicking, swiping, liking, following, and subscribing—determining who reigns, and who's ignored. But what does it mean to actually BE popular? Turns out, there is more than one type of popular.

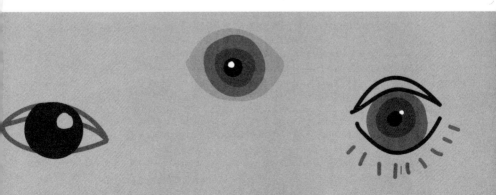

Chapter 1

Defining Popularity

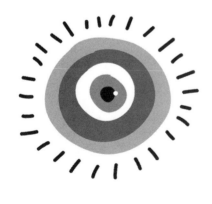

What does "popular" actually mean? The word "popular" comes from the Latin word *popularis*, meaning belonging to, devoted to, or accepted by the people. Basically, this meant "for ordinary people."[1] But of course, that's not the way we think about the word popular today.

What does popularity mean to you? How would you define this word? How do you know when someone is popular?

---

1   popular | Origin and meaning of popular by Online Etymology Dictionary. (2020). Etymonline.Com. https://www.etymonline.com/word/popular

Scientists who study popularity (yep—there are people who really study popularity for a living!) have identified two meanings for popularity. The first meaning is someone or something that is liked by lots of people, and disliked by few. The second focuses on reputation: who is most well-known, or has the highest social status...which often doesn't have much to do with who is well-liked at all.

What qualities describe the people that you like the most? Circle the qualities that are most important to you and add more of your own.

FUNNY	
ATTRACTIVE	
KIND	
GOOD AT SPORTS	
LAID BACK	
CONTROLLING	
ACCEPTING	
PUTS OTHERS DOWN	

What qualities describe the people that have the reputation for being the "most popular"? Circle the qualities that you first think of and add more of your own.

FUNNY	
ATTRACTIVE	
KIND	
GOOD AT SPORTS	
LAID BACK	
CONTROLLING	
ACCEPTING	
PUTS OTHERS DOWN	

The way these two types of popularity affect one another in the real world is pretty complex.

In this workbook, we will use different words to refer to each of these different types of popularity, to try and make it a little less confusing. One is called "likability" and the other is called "status." Likability is the quality of being readily and easily liked by others. Status is how widely known, influential, dominant, and powerful a person is. There are upsides and downsides to each type.

We're going to examine behaviors, trends, and outcomes of both types of popularity. And, hopefully, you'll learn something about yourself and the type of popular you want to be.

Why do you think it's important to be popular?

_____

_____

_____

_____

_____

TO SUM UP

- The definition of popularity has changed over the years—and will probably continue to change!
- There are two kinds of popular: likability (being well-liked by others) and status (being well-known and having influence).

CHAPTER 2

WHAT IS LIKABILITY?

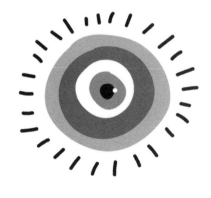

You probably didn't think much about popularity in kindergarten, but research shows us that young kids actually can be very popular or unpopular as early as age three. But at that age, it's almost exclusively the "likability" type of popularity. What does "likable" even mean?

Believe it or not, psychologists have done hundreds of scientific studies to understand what likability is, how to be likable, and how being liked by others affects you years later. The results from these studies tell us that likable kids have tons of friends, get lots of invitations to play, and are relied on by others to make decisions or rules about games and activities. How do they become so likable? It's a little complicated, because there may be a lot of reasons why we like someone. But overall, it seems that the most likable kids are the ones that make others feel happy, valued, and included when they are around. Let's break that down a little.

What do you like? How much would each of these attributes make you like someone?

	Not at all	A little	Somewhat	A lot
A good sense of humor; makes me laugh	1	2	3	4
Likes to do what I like to do	1	2	3	4
Makes me feel important to them; they want to be friends with me	1	2	3	4
Talks about themselves a lot	1	2	3	4
Has lots of followers on social media	1	2	3	4
Gets angry, even at the smallest things	1	2	3	4
Looks attractive	1	2	3	4
Helps me out when I need it	1	2	3	4
Has lots of energy and makes me feel excited about stuff	1	2	3	4
Smart	1	2	3	4
Thinks everyone else is kind of stupid	1	2	3	4

Recipe for Likability

INGREDIENTS FOR LIKABILITY:

Make others feel good
Make others feel valued
Make others feel included

· · · · · · · · · · · · · · · · · · ·

Recipe Yields:
Long-lasting relationships
Higher self-esteem
Long-term popularity

Sometimes hanging out with others makes us feel good. Sometimes it makes us feel worse.

Likable kids can make others happy in a bunch of different ways. What makes someone likable to you will vary depending on your age and interests. When you were in elementary school, the likable kids were the ones that made you laugh, had fun ideas for games to play, or had access to cool toys or places. As you got older, likable people are still the ones that make you laugh or have fun ideas, but they also say things that make other people feel good about themselves. And when we feel good when we are around someone, we start to feel like we want to spend more and more time with them. That's the first ingredient to making a person likable.

What is an example of a time when you felt happier after hanging out with someone?

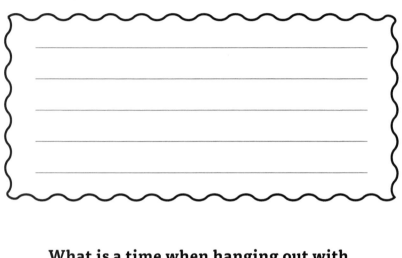

What is a time when hanging out with someone made you feel worse?

Likable people also make others feel valued. That's important, because we all know that there are some people we think are fun, but who we don't necessarily want to hang out with all the time. Sometimes we want to feel that we're important to someone who cares about us, has our back, and would pick us out of a crowd of people—someone we feel connected to. Likable kids are really good at making others feel that way and attracting people to them. Sometimes it's just something subtle that does it, like making eye contact or nodding to show that they are really listening. But likable kids also do a great job of trying to build on others' ideas to make them feel listened to and cared about. On the playground in elementary school, the unlikable kid who wants to play with trucks while everyone else is using Legos will say "Legos are stupid, let's ram these trucks together!" The likable kid will probably be a little more patient, play with the Legos, and then start building them into roads for trucks, guiding the group toward a whole new way to play that everyone ends up enjoying even more. Likable people tend to be more optimistic and less gossipy. They don't feel the need to take someone else down, because they feel secure in their relationships.

How do you make other people feel important?

The last ingredient to likability has to do with making people feel included. It's human nature to like people who like us, so whether we realize it or not, we're usually looking for signals to tell us whether someone is bringing us in or pushing us away. And when people invite others to hang out, or stick up for someone who is left alone, or pull up a chair in the cafeteria to let someone else join, or even tag a follower that they know would find a post funny, it makes them more likable because you know that it's safe to start to feel closer to them.

In contrast, being aggressive toward others has the exact opposite effect—it makes people feel that they are not wanted. For that reason, acting aggressively (fighting, name calling, spreading rumors, excluding others, teasing, etc.) is the single biggest predictor of being disliked.

What are some ways that other people have made you feel included?

(blank lined writing space)

The Likability Matrix

When psychologists do research to learn about likability, a common method is to ask students to look at a roster of everyone in the class or in

their grade, and then ask them two questions:
Who do you like the most? Who do you like the
least? Most kids (about 60%) are in the middle,
in the Average group (about an equal number
of people say they like them the most or least).
About 10-15% are considered Accepted (lots
of people say they like them the most, few say
they like them the least), 10-15% are Rejected
(many peers like them least, and few like them
the most), 10-15% are Neglected (rarely picked
for either question), and about 5-10% are
Controversial (some people really like them, and
some really don't, but most know them well).

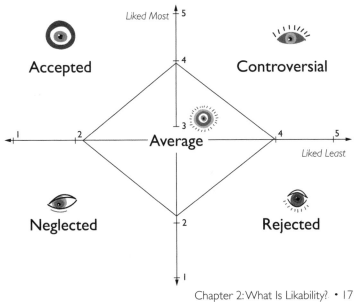

When studies look at what happens to kids in each of these groups, they find that kids who are Average or Neglected seem to be fine years later. Rejected kids are at higher risk for loneliness, depression, anxiety, or even substance use years later. Accepted kids tend to be the most likely to be happy, have many positive relationships, get good grades, and even get sick less often as they get older. As for the Controversial kids, well, they grow up to be more likely to develop the second form of popularity, which we'll talk about in the next chapter.

Check out these example scenarios:

 Accepted: Juan leads his team to victory each week on the soccer field because he is a strong leader who positively supports his teammates while holding himself to high standards on the field. He's outgoing and confident, but can own his mistakes and never feels the need to tear down his teammates. Juan exudes confidence, so others are drawn to him.

Controversial: Everyone knows who Donny is, and he kind of likes it that way. Whether he is trying to be the class clown in math, or doing things that make people laugh at him (sometimes with him!) during lunch, Donny is someone that everyone has strong feelings about. Some like him because being around Donny is a sure-fire way to get a lot of attention, and he is very aware of exactly which kids he can pick on to make himself stand out more. Other kids don't like him because they think he is superficial, immature, and sometimes a bully.

Average: Charleen is not on most people's radar at her school, but she has a great group of friends that enjoy her company. She can be funny sometimes and annoying at other times. She is invited to parties within her friend group, but not outside of it. She's happy, smart, and confident, and enjoys contributing to the conversation as well as sitting back and listening. Other classmates enjoy working on projects with her because she can lead a team without a lot of commotion. She stays away from social media to avoid the drama, but regularly texts with her group of friends.

 Neglected: There's nothing wrong with Maria. She's a little quiet, and those who know her think she is really sweet. But when people are thinking about who to invite to hang out, most kind of forget about Maria. She sits with one or two other kids at lunch who are similarly just not as well known, and rarely get much attention at all. They're not mean, or lame, or nasty, or funny. They are just regular kids who don't spend a lot of time speaking up or hanging out where others are.

 Rejected: Sarah tries so hard to be liked by others, but everyone is quick to say that she is one of the last people they would want to hang out with. Sarah is a little short-tempered and sometimes she acts in ways that don't fit the "vibe" of the room. Sometimes she speaks too loudly, or she acts too much like a little kid when everyone else is being serious, and sometimes she talks about music and movies that her peers don't like. At some point, other kids in her grade start calling her names and excluding her, and now no matter what she does—awkward or not—she is kind of socially toxic. People automatically disagree with whatever she says, because no one wants to be seen as similar to Sarah at all.

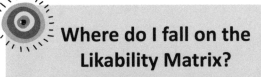

Where do I fall on the Likability Matrix?

Most of us think we know what others think of us, but we are wrong more often than we are right. Rather than trying to guess, we've put together a short quiz to help you uncover where you might fall on the Likability Matrix. If you're not sure, ask a friend to help you answer the following questions.

	Strongly disagree	Somewhat disagree	Neither agree nor disagree	Somewhat agree	Strongly agree
1. My peers would say that I am very well-liked by most other kids my age	1	2	3	4	5
2. I am often included in parties or social events	1	2	3	4	5
3. My peers would say that I am very disliked by most other kids my age	1	2	3	4	5
4. I have as many close friends as I want	1	2	3	4	5
5. Many kids my age make fun of me	1	2	3	4	5

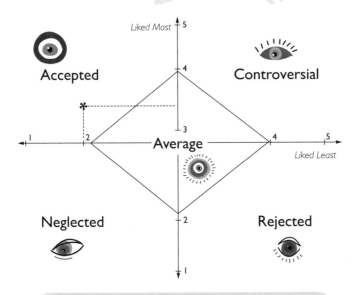

Accepted

Controversial

Average

Neglected

Rejected

Scoring: Plot your score on the matrix using the average of your scores from items 1, 2, and 4 onto the Liked Most line (vertical line) and the average of your scores from items 3 and 5 on the Liked Least line (horizonal line). For instance, the sample scores listed below would yield a Liked Most average score of 3.3 and a Liked Least average score of 2.

Item 1: 4
Item 2: 2
Item 3: 2
Item 4: 4
Item 5: 2

How do you feel about the likability group you are in? (No one's going to see this but you!)

Are you sure that's the group you're in? Can you think of any examples of things that happened with peers that tell you how much they like you, or not? Are there examples that might suggest the opposite?

Earlier, we discussed several things that can make people become more likable. If you're struggling with likability, what are three things you could do to be more likable to others? Get specific to your own life and experiences!

1.

2.

3.

If you really are stuck in the neglected or rejected category, don't worry! In the next section we will help you find a way into a new part of the matrix.

TO SUM UP

- Kids start paying attention to popularity as young as age three.
- Having likability comes from making others feel good, valued, and included.
- There are five main levels of likability: rejected, neglected, average, accepted, and controversial. Most people are in the average group (and we tend to be bad at knowing what others actually think of us!).
- People in the rejected and controversial groups can be at more of a risk for having trouble with social connections and self-esteem later in life; people in the average, accepted, and neglected groups are more likely to be confident and successful.

CHAPTER 3
WHAT IS STATUS?

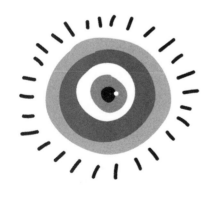

When you're in elementary school, there's no such thing as being "cool"—at least, not like there is in middle or high school. That's because as we get older, a second form of popularity emerges. It's called "status," and it's not about being likable at all.

This is probably an easy one:

What are some of the ways that having high status would feel good?

_____

_____

_____

_____

_____

_____

_____

_____

_____

Status is not the same as likability. In fact, about two-thirds of people who are high in status actually are among the most disliked kids in their grade.

But that doesn't seem to matter; kids high in status are called "popular" anyway. Being high in status means that a kid is known by pretty much everyone. They are dominant (which means that they are in charge), they set the rules for what is "cool," and they seem to be able to get away with anything. Status also comes with some power and influence, so as you've probably noticed, when high-status kids do something (enjoy a certain kind of music, wear a type of clothing, hang out at a specific place), it seems like everyone else wants to do the same thing.

What about some ways that it would be *tough* to have high status?

_____

_____

_____

_____

_____

_____

_____

_____

_____

_____

_____

_____

_____

_____

★ Recipe for High Status ★

INGREDIENTS FOR STATUS:

Attractive
Dominant personality
Willingness to be mean-spirited
Spend a lot of time keeping
themselves relevant to others

Recipe Yields:
Higher rate of depression, anxiety
and loneliness
Higher rate of addiction
Loss of jobs
Loss of relationships
Short-term popularity

Well, just like there's research on likability, there's also research on status, and there are a few factors that make people get this kind of attention and influence. First, high-status people are usually physically attractive. Second, high-status teens often are the people who act most like teenagers. In other words, they don't act like young kids and they don't act like adults. In fact, acting too much like an adult or like a little kid is one of the biggest predictors of *low* status. Third, sadly, being mean to others often makes kids have more status, which is why in movies and TV shows, the most popular kids are often depicted as the bullies. That's probably why high-status kids are often so disliked by so many people in their grade, though. Acting aggressively may make kids seem like they have more power, but it is the quickest way to become disliked.

These days, lots of people look for status not only at their schools, but also online. And gaining high status on social media doesn't work the same way as it does offline. Status on social media definitely has something to do with physical attractiveness too, but it also grows out of lots of social media activity, "liking" other people's posts, and creating content that people find funny, clever, or even controversial.

Social media seems to be designed specifically for status, rather than likability. Many platforms offer an opportunity for people to gain "friends" or followers, and for people to like posts, but really the emphasis is on the number of people you attract and not actually who they are, or developing a close relationship with them.

Think about the ways that social media focuses on status rather than likability. **What are some examples of this that you've seen?**

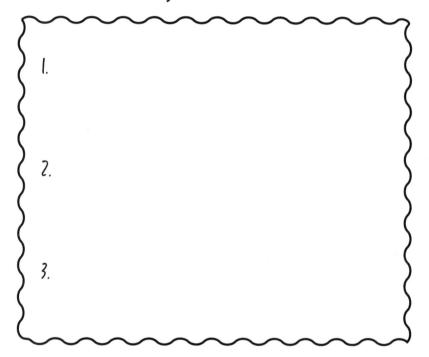

1.

2.

3.

Research studies designed to understand what happens to high-status people over time reveal a concerning picture. In contrast to all of the benefits of high *likability*, those high in *status* grow up at much higher risk for depression, anxiety, and loneliness. They are more likely than average-status and low-status peers to be fired or demoted at work. Also, high-status kids are at greater risk for drug addiction, and they tend to have serious problems with relationships. In one study, researchers found that kids high in status grew up to have friends and romantic partners who said they didn't actually want to spend much time with them (kind of defeats the point of having a partner, doesn't it?). They complained that the people who grew up with high status were still fixated on status years later, and they reported that they continued to be aggressive and to "use" people around them rather than being authentically connected. In another study, people high in status reported that they worry all the time about their status, and they couldn't trust when people wanted to hang out with them because they felt like people only wanted to be with them to get more status for themselves.

Which Type of Popularity?

Read each statement and decide if you think the person is looking for status or likability. Then think about why you think that. Sometimes people's intentions are obvious…but sometimes we need to stop and reconsider our first assumptions.

Jamie invites your friends to a sleepover but leaves you out. What may be her intent?

STATUS OR LIKABILITY?	HOW DO YOU KNOW?

Jon constantly posts YouTube videos of himself jumping off different structures. He spends much of his day refreshing his YouTube feed to see how many new views, likes, or subscribers he received.

STATUS OR LIKABILITY?	HOW DO YOU KNOW?

Rosita texts two of her friends and suggests that they meet to get frozen yogurt. When they arrive, someone suggests posting a selfie of them all together, and Rosita says, "Sure, if you want. But I kinda want to just have some time for us."

STATUS OR LIKABILITY?	HOW DO YOU KNOW?

Sometimes a person's intent is clear and sometimes it may be muddled. As humans, we are dynamic and complicated. You may have found that some of your answers felt straightforward; "yes, this is an example of status-seeking." Or "yes, this person is being inclusive and likeable." But other times, it's hard to tell. Maybe there are outside circumstances that stopped a person from inviting you, for example, like having a guest limit set by their parents. Don't worry! Life is full of these gray moments where the answer isn't clear. Where we all need to start is by acknowledging what we see right in front of us without prejudice or a preconceived idea about what the "right answer" may be. Once we can clearly see the situation in its entirety, we can hone in on how we want to handle it.

Maybe this seems pretty straightforward so far. The fact that some kids are likable, and some are popular, and those aren't always the same people, may not exactly be breaking news. In the next section we will discuss the science behind popularity and why so many seek status even though it comes at a cost. Understanding that information can help you see status-seeking and likability in a new light and give you new tools to deploy when you are in a complicated situation.

TO SUM UP

- "Status" is the more stereotypical type of popularity, but frequently the people highest in status do not actually have high likability.
- Status is often built on physical appearance, a dominant or aggressive personality, a willingness to put others down, and a high level of dedication to staying relevant.
- Much social media is built almost entirely on the idea of status.
- Long-term, high likability is a much better predictor for success and happiness; high-status people are more likely to develop depression, anxiety, and loneliness.

SECTION 2

WHY DO WE WANT IT?

Is it weird that everyone talks about popularity so much after elementary school? Is it strange that people spend so much time staring down at their phones—sometimes not even realizing that they are about to bump into someone or something? Why is popularity such a big deal?

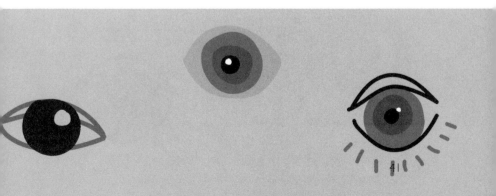

CHAPTER 4

THE SCIENCE BEHIND POPULARITY

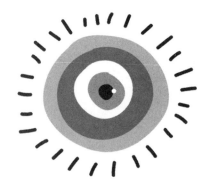

Before we begin to uncover the formula for becoming the right kind of popular, we need to understand the brain science behind what drives us to WANT to be popular in the first place.

Let's start with some examples to set the stage.

Rosie is sitting at home, alone and bored. She doesn't feel like watching a show, and no one is available to text. So she logs onto her social media account and posts something random. As she watches, the likes go from 0 to 3, then 10, then 19 over the next 30 minutes. She starts to feel better. "This doesn't really mean anything," she tells herself, but for some reason, whenever she needs a little boost, she does it again.

Kenny is popular, but he also is kind of a jerk. When he was a little kid, he used to play with his neighbor, Antwon. But kids say that Antwon is kind of a nerd now, so whenever he is near, Kenny calls him names loud enough so everyone can hear him and laugh. Kenny sometimes feels bad about teasing his old friend, but for some reason he keeps doing it. Something about the way everyone laughs with Kenny makes him feel good.

Deja knows that she looks good. She spends extra time every morning picking clothes that make her a trendsetter rather than a trend follower. She gets a lot of compliments when she walks around at school, and one day, she overheard a bunch of girls whispering about how they think she is the best-dressed girl in their school. Of course, Deja loved hearing that. She already knew she was a good dresser, but there was something about just knowing that other people were talking about her that made her feel really good.

The Brain Game

Rosie, Kenny, and Deja aren't weird for feeling the way they do. In fact, almost every pre-teen or teenager would feel the same way that they do—and they may even go out of their way to feel that way all of the time. That's because for most kids, at around the age of 11 something happens in our brains that makes us crave what scientists call "social rewards": that good feeling that people get when they think that others are admiring, imitating, agreeing with, or even just looking at them.

Here's why: everyone knows that their body changes in adolescence, right? But most don't know that a few years before their growth spurt, their brain starts to change too, and those changes happen one brain region at a time. One of the first changes is to the area that is related to how we feel in social situations—this area gets supercharged as brain receptors for two substances start to multiply. These substances are oxytocin (which drives us towards social connection) and dopamine (which makes us feel good), and the brain region is called the ventral striatum. And once we learn what makes it activate, nearby brain regions start leading us to have cravings, instincts, and preferences for more of what will make us feel good. We don't realize this is happening, of course—this is all in parts of our brain that work behind the scenes without us having to think about it consciously. And that makes it even more powerful.

This is why the "Like" feature on social media causes both joy and angst! When you get likes it's like getting a reward in your brain and you feel good. When you don't get likes, you may feel upset because you were denied the social accolades. This has become so problematic for young people that the creator of the "Like" button, Leah Perlman, regrets its creation, and now platforms like Instagram are making it so that only the account holder can see the number of likes, in an attempt to reduce some of the negative emotional impact the feature causes.

Ever wonder why you started feeling like everything your parents did was annoying and embarrassing around the ages of 11-14? Or why so many kids talk so much about who's popular, who's friends with whom, and who did what on social media? The answer is because our brains are built to make us want to become independent at around this age, and it does this by making us obsessed with our peers.

What kinds of things make you feel good? Are you sometimes craving those things more than you need? Does it ever get in the way of other stuff you should be doing?

_____

_____

_____

_____

_____

_____

_____

_____

_____

_____

_____

_____

What if it happened to you?

Which of the following things would feel pretty great if they happened to you? Check all that apply.

☐ Everyone laughed at a joke you made in front of the whole class.

☐ You started noticing that kids were dressing like you and talking like you.

☐ You were voted "Most Popular" by all the kids in your grade.

☐ Suddenly, you get 100 more followers on your Instagram account.

☐ Your friend group had to make a tough decision, and they listened to your idea.

☐ You were asked out for a date by three people in the same day.

☐ Your post something that goes viral.

☐ You are picked first to be on a team.

It's totally understandable if most or all of these things would feel great! Some might be less important to you personally, but these are all examples of social rewards that your brain is programmed to crave now. List a few more things here that would make you feel like people want to bond with you, follow you, pay attention to you, or would make everyone know who you were.

_____

_____

_____

_____

_____

_____

_____

_____

Reactions

Self-reflection: On a scale of 1-5, 1 being "I've never done this" to 5 being "I do this a lot," how often do you do each of the following things? The list on the next page are things some of us do daily, and others of us may not do at all. This reflection is to help you understand where you are and how you might want to change some of your habits or intentions. Some of these things may make you feel great about yourself and some might not feel good to admit, but try to be honest with yourself. That's the first step to making a change!

1.	Act friendly and nice to people you don't even know	1	2	3	4	5
2.	Post something funny online	1	2	3	4	5
3.	Wear clothes that are current and trendy	1	2	3	4	5
4.	Make a joke loud enough so other people can hear it	1	2	3	4	5
5.	Do something that's against the rules when others are watching	1	2	3	4	5
6.	Help out a kid who is in trouble	1	2	3	4	5
7.	Tease or gossip about a kid that no one really likes	1	2	3	4	5
8.	Say that something is boring or lame or say that you don't care about it, even when you do a little	1	2	3	4	5
9.	Post things to try and get more likes or followers	1	2	3	4	5

Scoring: Add up your scores for items 2, 3, 4, 5, 7, 8, and 9. Lower scores (out of 35 total) suggest that you don't let your cravings for social rewards change your behavior too much and you are not frequently mean to others. Higher scores suggest that you may be a bit status obsessed. In other words, you may be letting your desire to feel popular get in the way of other things you can be doing that may be better for you.

It's important to think about how your actions make other people feel, too. Circle the response that best fits for you.

Behavior	How does this make other people feel?	How often do you do this? (Use your score from earlier)	How do you feel when you do this? (1 = Terrible; 5 = Terrific)
Act friendly and nice to people I don't even know	Good Neutral Bad		1 2 3 4 5
Post something funny online	Good Neutral Bad		1 2 3 4 5
Wear clothes that are current and trendy	Good Neutral Bad		1 2 3 4 5
Make a joke loud enough so other people can hear it	Good Neutral Bad		1 2 3 4 5
Do something that's against the rules when others are watching	Good Neutral Bad		1 2 3 4 5
Help out a kid who is in trouble	Good Neutral Bad		1 2 3 4 5
Tease or gossip about a kid that no one really likes	Good Neutral Bad		1 2 3 4 5
Say that something is boring or lame or that you don't care about it, even when you do a little	Good Neutral Bad		1 2 3 4 5
Post things to try and get more likes or followers	Good Neutral Bad		1 2 3 4 5

Pretty much everyone has the urge to feel good when they are around others their age.

What are some things you want to do more of to feel good?

_____

_____

_____

_____

_____

Anything you want to do less?

_____

_____

_____

_____

_____

TO SUM UP

- At around the age of 11, our brains begin to make us crave what scientists call "social rewards."
- At the same time, the brain begins to produce more oxytocin, which makes us want to bond with our peers.
- Our brains are built to make us want to become independent at around this age, and it does this by making us obsessed with peers.

CHAPTER 5

STATUS WITHIN STATUS

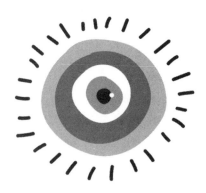

Categorizing people is a ubiquitous part of culture. By the time you're in high school, you've probably had a lot of experience with it—both seeing it and doing it yourself! We put people in boxes based on our own perceptions. For example, at school there are the athletes, socialites, academics, loners, and attention-seekers (there are probably many other categories, but let's just start here). While specific groups may seem more popular than others, popularity also exists within each group, with some individuals having higher status or being more likable than others.

There is often a power dynamic that exists within a group where some individuals have more influence over others. There are *leaders* (those in charge), *followers* (those happy to go along), *floaters* (those who don't have a set position as they tend to move from group to group with ease) and *on the fringe* (those who aren't really a central part of the group but are more on the periphery).

As humans, we have a tendency to label others and also label ourselves. We tend to select a group that we feel best fits our own label or the label we want to be a part of, and then act in ways that will help us fit in. We conform. Maybe the goal is influence and status, obsessing over virtual likes, subscribers, and views. Or maybe it is just being liked, admired, or accepted. Most of the time, people just want to be seen as worthy of others' attention. So we try different tactics. Some people may try on different personalities while others try on different outfits. At the heart of it, they're all just trying to find connections. It's the way we go about making those connections that determines what type of popular we will be.

That's where our own actions really start to matter! What role do we want to play in our group? What will we do in order to achieve the role we desire? Are we willing to share a leadership role, or is the idea of giving up the position unthinkable? Is our whole self-worth tied to our ability to maintain our status? Do we choose to create a space where others' feelings and desires matter as much as our own?

Status Within Status

Where do you fit? What role do you play? Fill in the top row of the chart on the next page with categories (our earlier examples included loners, athletes, academics, etc., but feel free to create your own). Then:

1. Add your name in the box(es) corresponding with your category and position (we know you are a multidimensional person who may or may not fit into multiple groups, so add your name in as many places as apply to you).

2. Add the names of others who you think fit these roles. They can also go in as many boxes as you want.

3. Under each name, add a few words about the traits of the person you see in each position of each category. For example, you may put yourself in the box corresponding with Athlete/Leader, then under your name, add the qualities that make you a good leader of your team. Feel free to do this on another sheet of paper if you need more room!

Category				
Leader				
Follower				
Floater				
Fringe				
Not Affiliated				

What do you notice about the traits people in different roles have? What traits are common to leaders, or loners, or whatever your groups may be?

Carlos, Sofie, Annika, Mateo, Maddie, Ravi and Anthony belong to a social justice club at school. Carlos and Sofie started the club their freshman year and now as juniors have created a club with influence! As the club has grown, it's gained members who are passionate about different social justice issues, and there are varying opinions about how and where their resources should be spent. This has caused some discourse. When Ravi joined the club last year, he brought to light that not a lot of attention was paid to his Indian community, their needs, and the discrimination they faced. Because Carlos and Sofie started the club, they felt that as leaders, it was their role to ultimately decide how the group spent their time and money. But Ravi was well-liked and respected by the other members of the group, and they wanted to support his initiatives. This led to the group feeling fractured and at odds. While everyone came in with the best of intentions, the social dynamic made it difficult to get things done and make decisions. Mateo, who had always been willing to go along with Carlos and Sofie in the past (a true and dedicated follower) spoke up and asked to make room for Ravi to explore social justice issues with the group so they could decide together. Carlos and Sofie reluctantly agreed.

The teacher was surprised by Carlos and Sofie's reaction and asked them why it was difficult to allow Ravi to bring a cause important to him to the group. The response was simple: they thought their ideas were better and felt that because they started the club, it was on them to make the final decision. However, in the end, they acquiesced. They accepted that in order to be truly inclusive (which was one of the causes they were fighting for as a social justice club) they needed to share their power.

When thinking about group dynamics, it's important to remember that a group can be just that: dynamic! Roles can change, temporarily or permanently. A leader is only as strong as their ability to listen, inspire and connect. Sometimes that means stepping back to let others take the lead. Someone only obsessed with status cannot be true leader, but just a big ole bossy pants!

When we begin to look at the social dynamics of a group and the roles that are played, it is important to remember that all roles come with pre-conceived notions, but it doesn't mean it has to be that way. By examining the character traits you associate with each role, you can begin to adopt those traits and grow into the role you feel is truly your best fit.

TO SUM UP

- Peer groups are their own microcosm, with people playing many different roles.
- The roles we play in any group can be dynamic (roles can change).
- Understanding the character traits associated with each role can help you uncover which traits you already posses or want to strive to attain in order to find your best fit.

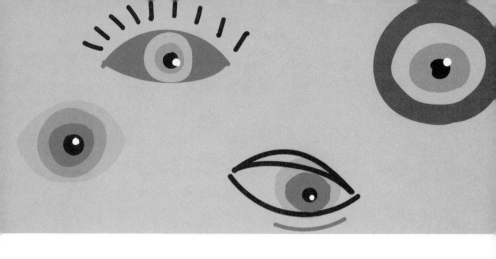

SECTION 3

HOW DID THEY GET IT?

Do you ever look at celebrities and influencers and wonder, "How did they get so popular?" Probably! Most of us have. But not all celebrities came to fame in the same way, or use their influence in the same way. In this section, we will look at how some famous people got their popularity, how popularity can be used, and the power of having such status.

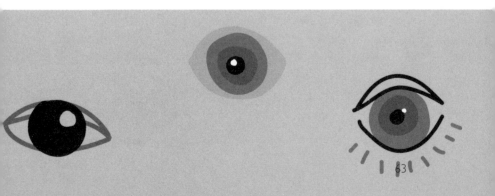

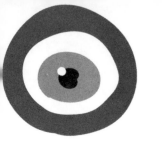

Chapter 6

HOW CELEBRITIES
FIND POPULARITY

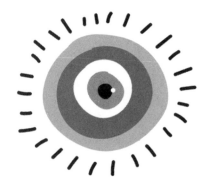

Celebrities, famous athletes, and others in the spotlight are a great case study for us to examine the effects of the different types of popularity. So much of what they do is right in front of us to judge or admire, but most of all we can learn from their outcomes.

Who is popular and how did they get that way?

Name three celebrities or influencers you feel are popular. What type of popularity did they achieve and how did they get it? (You might know some people's stories, but you might have to look some up! If you find out anything that's surprising, include that in your description.) You can use the chart on the next page for this, or another sheet of paper if you need more room.

Name of celebrity or influencer			
What type of popularity did they achieve?			
How did they get that way?			
How do you feel about their behaviors and their popularity?			
What kind of criticism has this person had to cope with?			
What may be some of the downsides to this celebrity's fame?			

Some high-profile people have gone to great lengths (even dangerous ones) to maintain their status, while others focus on being the best role-model they can be, understanding they are in the public eye. Check out these next examples. What type of popularity did they get? How did they get it?

Logan Paul became famous when his Vine videos began going viral in 2014. Paul was best known for his big stunts, where he purposely made a fool of himself in public doing dangerous, attention-seeking activities. Paul moved to YouTube (when Vine became defunct) and he continued his antics, sometimes taking them too far. His most controversial video came out in 2017, when he filmed himself visiting a Japanese "suicide forest" where he made fun of the custom and exposed millions of children to graphic images of suicide. He lost sponsors, but not his popularity.

Kylie Jenner was first introduced to us in 2007 on *Keeping Up With the Kardashians* when she was just 10 years old. The audience was charmed and shocked by the precocious child who spun on a stripper pole in the first season (a scandal at the time, which let the audience know that Kylie was not going to remain in the background for long). Since then, Kylie has made her own name in the world of influencers, launching her popular line of cosmetics that has made her a billionaire and a role-model in the world of entrepreneurship. Although her following is in the hundreds of millions, she is not immune to criticism. She was heavily and publicly shamed in 2019 after throwing a *Handmaid's Tale* party for a friend where they dressed in handmaid costumes (a symbol of both male-dominance and a woman's inability to control what happens to her own body), during a time when states were passing legislation that took away women's rights to their own bodies.

Cristiano Ronaldo is one of the greatest soccer players of all time and one of the most marketable athletes. With more than 172 million Instagram

Fame:
Being known or talked about by many

Attention-seeking:
Doing something to keep all eyes on you

Influencer:
Someone well-known enough that they can "influence" trends; often paid to spread information about popular products and events

followers, Ronaldo is a leading influencer. He rose to stardom through soccer and has been able to successfully capitalize on his fame and fortune while simultaneously promoting a list of philanthropic efforts as impressive as his 400+ goal count. Cristiano has turned his charm, good looks, and athleticism into an empire where his fame and popularity reach every demographic. But no matter how positive or even altruistic a person may be, under the microscope of fame, every action (both on and off the field) has the potential to be captured shared. Even Ronaldo has had to deal with his fair share of controversy, a price all celebrities seem to pay.

These three celebrities all came to fame in different ways, but there is a common thread: large groups of people are fascinated by their every move! While they are all popular, there are some glaring differences in the types of popularity they have achieved.

Downsides of fame?

Now think about these questions:

	Logan Paul	Kylie Jenner	Cristiano Ronaldo
What kind of criticism has this person had to cope with?			
Are people attracted to their image or to who they really are?			
What may be some of the downsides to their fame?			

Consequences of Celebrity

Psychological scientists have talked with celebrities to find out what it's really like to be famous. Some of what they found won't surprise you: people high in status get lots of attention, a bunch of free stuff, tons of followers, and sometimes millions of fans.

Research also discovered some unexpected things. Celebrities are often pretty lonely. They work so hard to cultivate an "image," but then report that they lose sight of who they really are, as compared to who everyone thinks they are. They also have so many people wanting to be near them, and wanting to get the same perks as them, that many start doubting who their real friends are, and who is just using them for their fame. Slowly, many celebrities close off their social circles to fewer and fewer people that they trust, all while feeling that people only liked them for their status, and not for the person that they really are inside. Research shows that many famous people crave and love their fame, but start to feel like they don't actually have many people they can talk to in a real way, or places they can go without getting unwanted attention. A large number of people with high status end up wishing that they didn't have it. Or, to put it a different way, they end up just wanting what highly likable people have.

TO SUM UP

- Some celebrities and influencers are intentionally trying to achieve status popularity and will do just about anything to get it.
- Other celebrities and influencers are more interested in sharing their talents and become popular due to their high likability.
- It is not necessary to beg for likes, views or subscribers, give up your self respect, or put others down in order to achieve fame. Talent, character, and likability can produce the same results.
- People with high status often feel lonely, misunderstood, and untrusting of others.

CHAPTER 7

THE ROLE OF INFLUENCERS

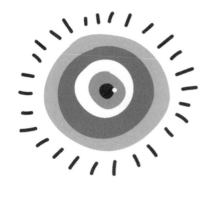

It's easy to fall for status—especially today when the online community is all about achieving exactly that! When YouTube pays you money for reaching a certain number of audience members and influencers are constantly bombarding their audience with pleas of "subscribe, like, or follow," it is common for people to focus on the wrong kind of popularity. In this section, we want you to reflect on the more positive aspects of individuals you admire and why.

We asked 200 college students what they thought about social media influencers. As you can see, they had mixed feelings, and very few thought it was a good idea for young people to be influenced by them.

Do influencers do more good or more harm to our society in general?

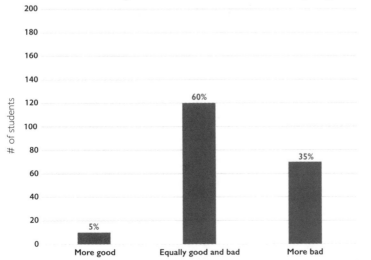

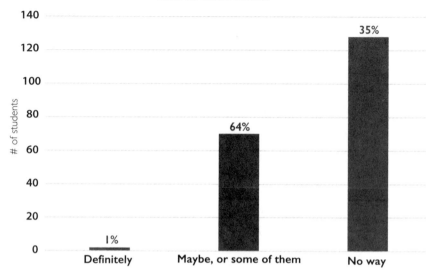

Would you want your own children to follow influencers such as these online?

Status makes us feel good. When we look at our profiles and see that we have dozens or even hundreds of likes, it makes our brains release dopamine, which makes us feel rewarded. But have you noticed how long that feeling lasts? For most of us, it's just a few minutes—and then we need to do it again if we want to keep feeling good. That's a problem when we get addicted to the rewarding feeling; we spend far more time than we realize online to try and capture that feeling for a little longer.

What makes someone a good social media user?

Social media can be incredibly positive or horribly disastrous, and much of it has to do with YOU, the user. Circle all of the personality traits, characteristics, or skills a user should have in order to have more positive experiences than negative with social media. Add some of your own in the blank spaces, too.

CONFIDENT   JEALOUS   FEARS MISSING OUT   SENSITIVE

EASILY INFLUENCED   DISCERNING   GULLIBLE   PEOPLE-PLEASER

KIND   TECH-SAVVY   RELATIONSHIP-SEEKING   ASSERTIVE

OPINIONATED   THOUGHTFUL   ORGANIZED   CONTROVERSIAL

_____   _____   _____   _____

Sometimes our fixation with status gets even stronger when we see people who have a ton more followers than we have. We imagine, even if just for a second, what it would be like to have so many people like what we say or how we look, and respond to what we post with messages of love, support, and attention.

There are two important factors to consider when it comes to online influencers: how they came to be an influencer to YOU, and how your brain interprets what you are seeing.

Who, in your real life, do you admire? What qualities do they possess?

Influencers can be passed on to you as a recommendation from a peer or family member, but more often than not, it's an algorithm making a decision about who might influence you. An algorithm is a process or set of rules to be followed. Social media platforms use this process to make recommendations to you. For example, have you ever watched a YouTube video and then YouTube makes a recommendation (or autoplay just starts the next video) and you're like, "Oh! I totally want to watch that!"? It's not a coincidence. YouTube makes these recommendations based on other videos you've watched, Google searches you've conducted, and your social media posts, comments, and likes. The internet pays attention to everything we do in order to theoretically make our online experience better and more personalized, including sending influencers to our feed. While it's great that we are fed things of interest, it can also be problematic when what we are being presented with makes us think that something is normal or true (when it may not be) just because it is being presented to us over and over again. Influencers are not vetted and are not required to tell the truth or consider how their channel or feed may affect their audience. So someone struggling with an issue can actually have their issue exacerbated. For example, say someone is struggling with their body image, and they search for ways to feel better about their body. That search might prompt the algorithm to send influencer content that discusses body image—but the messaging in that content may actually encourage unhealthy habits.

Sometimes these influencers can have a positive effect, and other times they can leave us feeling downright terrible about ourselves. You may not have been seeking out certain advice, but here it is, right in front of you, making you believe that you need to pay attention and admire.

There's something even more important to know, which is what that kind of admiration of others can do to our brains. Research studies have looked at adolescents' brains while on Instagram and platforms like it, and have discovered then when we see a ton of likes, it changes the way we think about things, without us even realizing it. In one study, results showed that when we see posts of something dangerous, our brains' "brakes" are activated—a region called the prefrontal cortex that keeps us from acting impulsively. That's good—it helps keep us safe. But when those same images of dangerous situations are shown with *a lot of likes attached*, the brain's brakes don't activate at all. Just seeing that others have liked an image actually changes the way we think about things, and soon we are being influenced by others without us even realizing it.

This is why it's so important that we pay attention to who may be influencing us online. Are our thoughts, feelings, opinions, or behavior being influenced in ways we don't expect? Who would you prefer to be influenced by instead?

Who do you follow online (just pick a couple)? Why? What qualities do these people possess that attracts you to their feed, story, or channel?

Ask your parents who they emulate and admire and why.

Are their answers similar or different to yours (in qualities, if not specific people)?

Ask your closest friends, too (you may already know some of their answers!).

Who do they emulate and admire? Why?

_____

_____

_____

_____

_____

_____

_____

_____

_____

_____

_____

_____

_____

_____

Do you notice any patterns? Do you follow any of the same people, or at least people with the same qualities, as your friends or parents? You probably follow some people who are more status-obsessed than likable, but hopefully you follow some because they seem like positive, encouraging people. How do these people express themselves differently? How do they use their fame and influence in a positive way?

_____

_____

_____

_____

_____

_____

_____

_____

_____

_____

You As an Influencer

If you could be an influencer, what type of influencer would you be? What sorts of qualities would you want to share with the world? How could you do it?

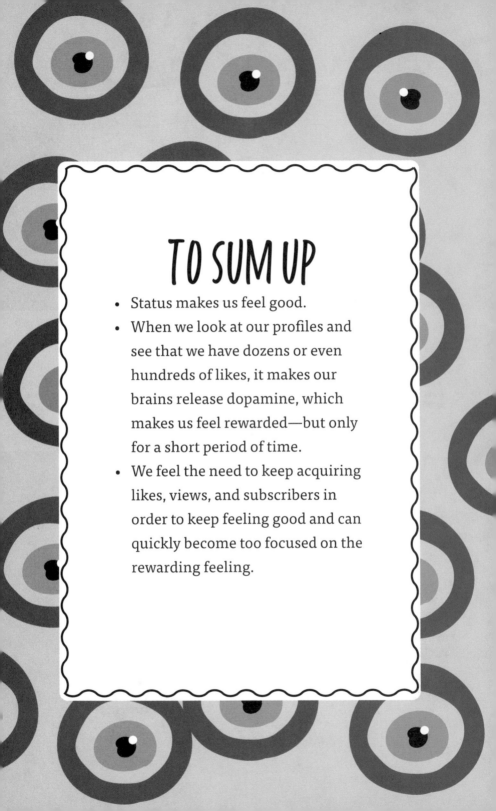

TO SUM UP

- Status makes us feel good.
- When we look at our profiles and see that we have dozens or even hundreds of likes, it makes our brains release dopamine, which makes us feel rewarded—but only for a short period of time.
- We feel the need to keep acquiring likes, views, and subscribers in order to keep feeling good and can quickly become too focused on the rewarding feeling.

Chapter 8

POWER AND STATUS

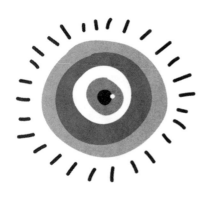

Now that you have a better understanding of the different types of popularity, have reflected on your role and social standing, and have looked at how celebrities have garnered popularity, it's time to look at the role power plays in status.

Status-seekers often use tactics that may make them disliked but at the same time raise their status. Some people discover that when someone else REALLY wants to be friends with them, they can use that to their advantage. Being mean to others sometimes makes them work harder for approval, which gives power to the person being mean. This power dynamic seems to favor the status-seeker, but over time, this tactic often leads the status-seeker to confuse power for a real relationship.

Let's take a look at what happens when status is used to control and manipulate. Sometimes popularity can feel so important, interactions with status-popular kids may convince people to do something they know is a really bad idea. Read the following story and keep an eye out for the types of popularity and actions we talked about.

Jack is popular! He is at the center of everyone's social universe and has been since kindergarten. He is funny and articulate, well-liked by teachers and parents, and feared by most of his classmates. Jack can turn on the charm in one moment and destroy the self-esteem of a peer in the next. He has power.

Who are three people in your grade or in your school who have that kind of power? What do they do to remind you that they are powerful?

At the beginning of the school year, Jack began sending messages to his classmates daring them to post photos or videos on SnapChat or TikTok doing something against the rules or illegal, like stealing from school or a store.

When his classmates refused (which most did), he asked if they were a goody-two-shoes, and threatened to spread a rumor about them. He taunted and manipulated his targets.

Although many of his peers had originally emphatically told Jack they were not interested in his games, he continued to wield his popularity over them, making them feel powerless in the situation. He badgered and coerced them with threats of exposing secrets and spreading rumors. Eventually, a handful of students complied, worried that NOT sending would do more damage to their own status.

Some of you are probably thinking, "What idiots!" Maybe you think he's the idiot, or maybe you think the kids who documented themselves breaking the rules are the ones who did something stupid, but whatever your first reaction may be, let's unpack the situation and look at the role popularity played.

Jack has status. Other kids want to be around him because it gives them status, too. If you are part of Jack's world you are at the center of everything. If you are on the outs with Jack, it can feel like you are a social pariah. It's miserable to be on the outside, so maybe giving up a bit of self-respect would be easier than dealing with the consequences of Jack's wrath.

Eventually, it got back to the principal. Some of the students who got caught said that Jack had been pressuring lots of people into it. Unfortunately, as commonly happens, even classmates who were not directly involved took sides, and many sided with Jack, claiming that the people who posted photos and videos had a choice.

One student, Mandy, who had sided with Jack, accosted one of the students who reported him, cursing and saying that they had thrown Jack under the bus. When Mandy was interviewed, she said, "They weren't forced to do anything!"

When the students directly involved (those who had been pressured by Jack) were interviewed, several students reported being terrified that if they didn't oblige, Jack would think less of them, and that was scary in and of itself.

The type of emotional warfare Jack waged against his targets can feel as threatening as physical violence. Although Jack may not have held their finger and pressed the send button for them, he gave his targets two choices: to post and stay in his good graces, or refuse and be isolated. It's easy to say from an outsider's perspective, "I would NEVER be that weak!" Maybe that's true, and that's great if you have the ability to stand up for yourself in this situation! But the fear of isolation from your peers can be a very powerful weapon that leads some people to head down a path they never imagined they would.

Have you done any of these things so you would not be targeted by more popular kids?

	Never	Sometimes	Often
Made fun of a kid that popular people also made fun of			
Posted something or liked a post that made fun of someone else			
Didn't stick up for someone when I could have, because I was afraid popular people would target me			
Did something risky or dangerous or stupid because I thought I might get targeted by popular kids if I didn't			
When I could have been nice, I just kind of dismissed someone because helping them may have affected my own popularity			
Wore specific clothes, a hairstyle, or said I liked a kind of music that I knew popular people would approve of			
Started talking or acting like popular kids to make me feel more like them			

This type of power play happens regularly in teen groups: the popular teen is able to use their status to control others and even convince them to give up their own self-respect to remain in the good graces of their peer group. The question becomes, what do you do about it?

What do you do when you feel powerless?

What might be some of the reasons Jack acted the way he did? Could there have been things in his own past that brought him to this moment? What do you think Jack was hoping to gain or achieve beyond seeing the photos and videos?

Why do you think Jack's targets felt powerless?

How did the decision of those who were not directly involved to side with Jack contribute to the power dynamic? Why do you think it was easier for them to blame the targets rather than the person with power?

What are some things that Jack's classmates could have said that would have been better?

What would you say if you were talking to Jack right now and were in this situation?

_____

_____

_____

_____

_____

_____

_____

_____

_____

_____

_____

_____

_____

_____

_____

_____

_____

_____

_____

Have you ever had your power taken away? What happened and how did you react? Do you think in the future you could react differently if the same situation occurred? If so, how?

If the entire group had stood up to Jack and told him his actions were cruel and unwelcome, Jack would have lost his power. That's not the way it happens most of the time—at least, not in real life. What we see on TV shows or in the movies where the "bully" is defeated in the end sounds great, but we rarely see it in real life. Here is what we do see...

We see gossip and rumors and drama. We see splinter groups that quietly pull away from the larger group where the drama is taking place. We see people side with the Jacks of the world, leaving the victims feeling alone and helpless.

Sometimes a few courageous souls may take a stand against the injustice. Sometimes bystanders (those not involved but aware of the situation) become upstanders (those who support the victim). Again, there isn't one particular outcome in these situations. So what do YOU do?

You can start by having honest conversations with friends about power dynamics and how they make you feel. You can ask your friends if they have ever had their power stolen. What would you want them to do for you? What would they want you to do for them? By recognizing these types of situations for what they are (an attempt at using popularity to strip others of feeling safe), you can begin to create a plan of how you might respond in the future. Using this workbook and talking with friends is a great place to start!

TO SUM UP

- Power dynamics can play a large role in decision-making.
- The concern of being ostracized by your peer group can make it difficult to stand up for yourself or others.
- Coercion and manipulation can be just as frightening as the threat of a physical attack.
- Sometimes it may feel easier just to go along with the group, but in the end, you have to decide what kind of person and friend you want to be. Do your actions match your perception of yourself?

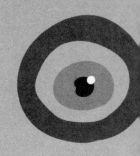

SECTION 4

WHY IS IT SO COMPLICATED?

There *is* a formula for success in popularity. But before we can teach you the formula, you have to decide what kind of popular is right for you. That starts with reflecting on what you did in the past, and whether it worked. If in the past you have obsessed over followers and likes, by now you've probably realized that even when you got them, it came with self-doubt and emotional rollercoasters. High highs when you received the positive feedback, and low lows when you received negative feedback or, maybe even worse, none at all.

Research has proven over and over again that this type of behavior does not lead to happiness and success. So if this WAS you but you're ready for something new, then stick with us to find out more.

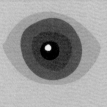

CHAPTER 9

CUE INTERPRETATION

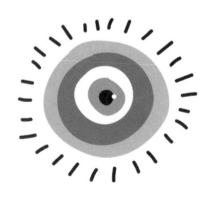

Ebony and Maria are eating lunch in the cafeteria. Tiffany, a popular girl in their grade, points to Ebony from across the room and shouts, "Hey Ebony, love the shirt!" There is an awkward silence at every table, and finally their classmates start talking again. Ebony is furious, and whispers to Maria that she can't stand how obnoxious Tiffany acts. Maria disagrees. "What are you talking about? You look great and Tiffany knows it!"

How could Ebony and Maria have such different takes on what Tiffany said? They both heard the same thing at the same time, and they both know a lot about Tiffany. But sometimes, even in the face of the exact same information (a text, a comment, or even a like) people can come to widely different conclusions about what it all means. Psychologists refer to this as "cue interpretations," which basically just means that we all have a different way of interpreting what we see and hear. In fact, we interpret hundreds of big and little social interactions every day. Most of the time, we all agree on what we think we experienced. But sometimes—especially if we are feeling sad, angry or scared—we have interpretations that are different from others'.

This is important because the way we interpret what we saw or heard usually leads to how we respond to others. In this instance, Ebony is ready to respond to Tiffany by calling her out for being rude. But Maria would more likely be friendly to Tiffany because she thinks her friend just got a genuine compliment.

Who is correct? We don't always know. But we do know that we all see the world through our own lens—like a filter or a bias—and it can start to mess with our relationships when we forget that we have our own unique way of interpreting social situations.

First Interpretation

In the chart below, write the first thing you think is happening—your first interpretation—for each of the social situations. Then, try and write a few more possibilities of what could be happening instead—even if you don't believe they are true at first.

Social Scenario	What's your first interpretation?	Any other possibilities?
I hear some friends talking about hanging out after school as I walk towards them. When they see me, they start talking about something else.		
A kid with a reputation for being mean is walking directly towards me at school. They are looking at me and smiling.		
An hour after a date, I get a text that says "☺ See ya"		
I posted a picture on Instagram after a new haircut. Two people have liked it since.		

Some people have a bias towards seeing people as being mean towards them, maybe a little more often than others. Other people see the world through "rose-colored glasses," missing out on signals that they may be in trouble. Still others may often assume that they are likely to be rejected or teased, even when they may not be. Everyone has one bias or another.

Your bias may have helped you at some point—for instance, being aware when people may be trying to hurt you might have helped keep you safe in elementary school when kids teased you a lot. But is this bias helpful still? Or did you maybe get stuck thinking about things in a way that you don't need to anymore? Maybe you don't need to assume that people are mean to you anymore....perhaps it's worth trying to look for more positive signs?

Similarly, maybe you are biased to think that people are always being nice to you because as a little kid, you had a ton of positive feedback. But maybe now you are missing subtle cues that people are giving you about some areas for improvement. Are you open to that feedback?

Take a look at your first interpretations.

Do you see any patterns? Do you expect or assume you will be rejected by others? Do you think you will always be accepted? Thinking about things like this can help you discover what biases you might be viewing social situations with.

_____
_____
_____
_____
_____
_____
_____
_____
_____

It's pretty common for people to assume the worst in their first interpretations. It's a defensive mechanism, putting ourselves on guard to protect ourselves. But when we don't learn to challenge those first pessimistic thoughts, it can end up really taking a toll on our relationships.

Take a look at some of your alternate interpretations. If you had a tendency to expect rejection at first, hopefully some of your alternatives are more positive! Can you convince yourself that they could possibly be true? It may be easier if you imagined one of these scenarios happened to your best friend instead, and you were trying to convince them your alternate interpretation was true instead.

What would you say to them?

We all have a bias in how we interpret social scenarios. That's natural.

Why do you think that you have the biases you do? Do they come from some real experiences you've had before? Are they similar to the biases of people around you?

Do you think having that bias could actually be helpful sometimes? How?

_____

_____

_____

_____

_____

_____

_____

_____

_____

_____

_____

_____

_____

_____

_____

_____

How might it be hurting your relationships?

How can you remind yourself to think of alternate interpretations next time? Are there clues in how you feel (really upset!) or things you do (start writing lots of texts with exclamation points!) that could serve as a signal to you that you may have jumped to one conclusion and forgotten to consider alternate interpretations?

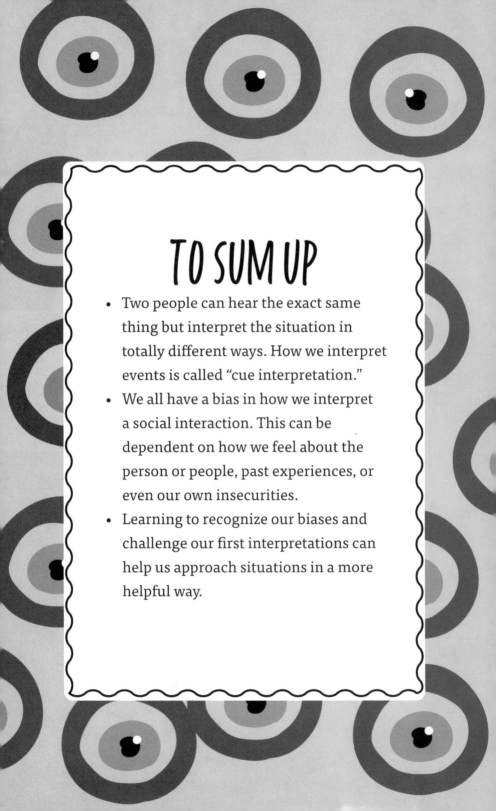

TO SUM UP

- Two people can hear the exact same thing but interpret the situation in totally different ways. How we interpret events is called "cue interpretation."
- We all have a bias in how we interpret a social interaction. This can be dependent on how we feel about the person or people, past experiences, or even our own insecurities.
- Learning to recognize our biases and challenge our first interpretations can help us approach situations in a more helpful way.

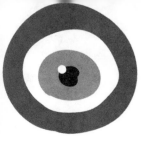

Chapter 10

Self-Esteem vs. Peer-Esteem

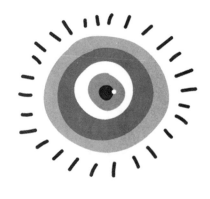

Uncovering the formula for becoming the right kind of popular also depends on understanding the differences between self-esteem and peer-esteem in order to increase self-worth. Let's define all three terms.

Before we discuss it, how would you define self-esteem?

Self-esteem is having respect for yourself or a positive impression of yourself. It is the way we evaluate ourselves (kind of an internal assessment of our qualities). When people have an unrealistic sense of who they are, it can lead to their self-esteem being either too high or too low. People who believe everything they do is amazing and wonderful and that everyone wants to know about it have a favorable but unrealistic impression of themselves: their self-esteem is too high. Then there are those who have very low self-esteem and believe that everything they do is terrible or wrong or unfavorable. Do you know people who post about every little thing they do? Like informing everyone about their breakfast burrito or bathroom habits? Interestingly enough, this over-sharing can come from both extremes of self-esteem! At the high-end of self-esteem, they think everyone wants to know what they ate for breakfast, and that their bathroom habits are the funniest thing in the world. And at the opposite end, the person may be looking for validation that burritos are a good breakfast choice, or that they can make people engage with them through something funny or shocking. And sometimes they're simply trying to act as if they think they're important in order to mask insecurity.

The term self-worth is often used interchangeably with self-esteem, but these are two different (but related) concepts. Self-worth is the belief that you are worthy of respect and consideration. It is possible to have low self-esteem but still believe you are worthy of someone's attention. But usually, as an individual works on building self-esteem, self-worth closely follows.

Peer-esteem is a little more complicated. Peer-esteem is the regard in which a peer holds another individual (basically, how others feel about you). Too often, people are overly focused on peer-esteem and not nearly enough on their own self-esteem. And when someone is too focused on gaining the approval of a peer, it may lead them down a path where they give up their own self-respect and cause both self-esteem and self-worth to dissipate.

What is a healthy way to feel good about yourself? For example, exercise, eating well, or setting a goal are all healthy ways to develop self-worth. What are some things you would enjoy doing?

Self-Worth Follow Up

After you've picked some healthy ways to feel good about yourself, use this table to log when you complete each action and how it made you feel.

Action	When you complete the action	How did it make you feel?
Example: Exercised for one hour	Daily	I always feel better about myself after I am done. I have energy and I seem to be nicer to my sister ☺

Have you ever watched a five-year old beg for the attention of a parent? They scream, "Look at me, look at me, look at me!" while they bounce on a trampoline or just pick their nose. The parent might be in the middle of a conversation, so they look over their shoulder and reply, "That's great sweetheart" without much affection or sincerity in their voice. Why? Because in that moment, the thing the child is doing isn't really worth watching and most definitely does not require feedback. The parent is accidentally feeding the idea that children should only want to do things if someone else is paying attention to them, rather than learning that they should do things they enjoy and are proud of. And if someone happens to notice, that's great, but it's not the intent.

This scenario, while it may seem normal and trivial, is a great jumping off point to understand how to develop quality self-esteem. Imagine if instead of the child screaming, "look at me, look at me, look at me!" as they bounced on the trampoline, they bounced and tried new tricks because they wanted to, not because they are waiting for a "good job" from someone else. Imagine if that parent then had an opportunity to look over and see their child's hard work and perseverance organically and paid the child a REAL compliment! This is a much better version of healthy attention. The child works at something and then feels good about their own accomplishment, and the compliment they receive isn't forced but honest.

The strong need for the "good job" is the precursor to online likes, views, and subscribers as kids get older. It becomes deeply engrained that without the feedback, what you just did wasn't worth doing in the first place. But that's just not true, and it doesn't build self-esteem. Trying new things, setting a goal and accomplishing it, and doing something nice for yourself or others are all things that promote self-esteem and build confidence at the same time.

A frequent question when it comes to this topic is "Does that mean that it's bad to get compliments?" And the answer is absolutely NOT! Compliments feel great! And they feel even better when you didn't go fishing for them in the first place. You just need to put it all in the right order.

SELF-ESTEEM +

SELF-WORTH +

PEER-ESTEEM

=

HEALTHY ATTENTION!

Let's take an athlete for an example. Tegan plays high school basketball. He's an amazing point guard and has already heard from college scouts. Tegan practices constantly. He studies the game and other players. When he is on the court he is laser-focused. When asked "Why do you play?" his first response is always the same: he loves the game. He loves the sense of accomplishment. And he appreciates the fans.

Notice that Tegan didn't say, "I love having fans!" He said he appreciates them. Tegan understands that while the accolades feel great, it's not the reason he does what he does. He works hard at his craft, which makes him feel that he has earned the respect of his teammates and coach (self-worth) and then he appreciates when his fans come out and cheer him on (the cherry on the sundae, so to speak), which is the peer-esteem. All that together increases his self-esteem. When you get the order right, you get a happy, emotionally healthy, and confident person.

Can you identify someone you know in real life that you see as a confident person? What is it about their behavior that makes you believe they are confident (how do they walk, talk, act, etc.)?

So let's look at confidence next. Confidence is the knowledge that you and the things you do are relevant and even important, but confidence doesn't always *require* peer-esteem. Have you ever noticed how a truly confident person behaves? We're not talking about those over-confident people who think everything they do is amazing, we're talking about people who walk tall, look others in the eye (even strangers), and smile as if the whole world is at their feet. Likability and confidence often go hand in hand. A confident person doesn't feel the need to control or put down others. They already feel good about their actions (healthy self-esteem), they respect themselves and others (healthy self-worth) and they appreciate their relationships (healthy peer-esteem). They don't feel the need to play games and hurt someone else in the process.

So how do you begin to develop a healthy sense of self that combines self-esteem and peer-esteem? It starts with understanding what these terms mean to you and reflecting

on your own actions. Here are a few things
healthy things you can do to raise your self-
esteem and self-worth:

- Participate in activities that make you
  feel good.
- Exercise or play a sport.
- Accomplish a goal or task.
- Remind yourself that everyone, including
  you, is worthy of respect.
- Aim for and prioritize meaningful
  connections with friends and peers.
- When you share things about yourself, share
  things you're truly proud of...not just your
  breakfast burrito!
- And perhaps most important, try and be as
  authentic as possible, so when people like
  you, they like the real you, and not a version
  of you that you have to work to make
  seem real.

TO SUM UP

- Self-esteem is having respect for yourself or a positive impression of yourself.
- Peer-esteem is the regard in which a peer holds another individual (how others feel about you).
- Self-worth is the belief that you are worthy of respect and consideration.
- Self-worth cannot be derived from peer-esteem alone.
- Self-esteem, self-worth, and healthy attention are key to a happy, confident person.

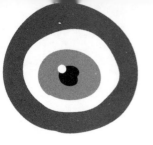

CHAPTER 11

COMPLICATED RELATIONSHIPS

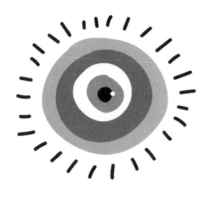

Sometimes, trying to develop self-worth can be difficult if you are in a complicated relationship. Maybe you feel powerless and put too much stock in what another person thinks about you. Have you ever considered if your self-worth is being manipulated by someone else? Or is it possible that you are the manipulator?

There is a term called "grooming" that is most often associated with personal safety and stranger-danger issues; however, this term can also apply to teens and their online and real-life relationships.

Grooming is a process by which an individual normalizes certain topics or behaviors in order to gain the trust and loyalty of another person. The online predator who convinces a child they are in a relationship is the most common tale of grooming, but let's look at how it can happen with a "friend." With peers, the grooming can be very subtle. The manipulator will build up the individual one day only to tear them down the next, thus normalizing the up and down roller-coaster relationship. This way the manipulator begins to break down your self-worth in exchange for their peer esteem.

Troy and Devon are "best friends"—or at least this is what they say. However, there seems to be a pattern in their friendship. When the two of them are alone, everything is great. They play video games, basketball, watch videos on YouTube, and hang out on the weekends around the pool. In these moments, both boys feel accepted by the other. They enjoy each other's company and have a lot in common.

But there is a power dynamic that doesn't always work in Troy's favor. When they are at school and Devon is with his "popular" friends, he teases Troy in front of the other guys. Devon puts him down, yells at him, and makes fun of him behind his back. Troy tries so hard to be the person Devon wants him to be so he doesn't embarrass himself or Devon in front of the group. However, no matter what Troy does, he constantly feels rejected by his "best friend" in these moments.

When Troy tries to talk to Devon about this in private, Devon tells him he is overreacting and to stop being so sensitive. Now Troy feels completely confused and unsure as to how he should be feeling. Troy tries other ways to make Devon happy; he buys him baseball cards, packs an extra special snack that they can share at lunch, and invites Devon to football games and other sporting events. Devon is always nice to Troy when Troy does something for him, which makes Troy feel like he is FINALLY being accepted by his best friend…only to have Devon knock him down again the next day at school.

Sometimes Devon will text Troy really funny memes (so Troy feels good about their friendship) and then 10 minutes later, Devon will send a group text including Troy with a meme that is meant to make fun of him (and Troy, once again, feels rejected).

No matter how long this goes on, Troy is constantly forgiving Devon and trying to win back his attention and friendship. At this point, Devon's emotional abuse leaves Troy vulnerable to participating in risky and even possibly dangerous behavior in order to please Devon. This is how grooming works. Devon is manipulating Troy and creating a push-pull game whereby Troy is constantly working hard for Devon's approval, thus giving Devon total control over Troy.

Has this ever happened to you? Try this exercise to determine if you are being groomed by a peer and may not even realize it. Is the relationship causing you to do things you know you shouldn't do? Do you feel powerless in the relationship?

How do your relationships make you feel?

Identify a specific person and think about specific interactions with them. How did these interactions make you feel? Did you feel accepted (regarded favorably), rejected (dismissed or inadequate), neutral (no feeling about the situation), or unsure (uncertain)? Looking for these patterns can help you identify healthy and potentially unhealthy relationships.

Here's an example:

Person's name or initials _____ JANE DOE _____

What happened?	When did it happen?	How did you feel?
Raven (a mutual friend) texted me a screen shot of Jane saying I was annoying	Tuesday	Rejected
I invited Jane to my house for a sleepover and she said YES!	Thursday	Accepted
We had a great time at the sleepover	Saturday	Accepted
At lunch she ditched me to sit with someone else and I ended up eating in the library	Monday	Rejected

Now it's your turn. Over the next few days pay close attention to interactions with peers and how they make you feel. You can log those exchanges in the table below.

Person's name or initials: _____

What happened?	When did it happen?	How did you feel?

After looking at the interactions, do you see a pattern? Do you think it's possible you are being manipulated, abused, or even groomed by a person? Keep in mind that one or two problematic interactions with a friend doesn't necessarily mean you're being manipulated, abused, or groomed. Sometimes even good, supportive friends have fights or misunderstandings. But if there's a long-term, recurring pattern of interactions that make you feel insecure or bad about yourself, it's time to think hard about whether this relationship is healthy.

A big part of developing healthy relationships is looking at how you are treated. Do you need to make changes to your relationships? Is it time to break away from a person trying to manipulate you? What could be holding you back from breaking off the relationship?

How do you think others feel in relationships with you?

Now it's time to take a hard look at how you may be treating others. While it may or may not be intentional, sometimes when we feel manipulated, we turn around and do the same thing to someone with less power. Sometimes it is a younger sibling, or maybe a friend you had in elementary school that you don't really hang out with anymore but who you know would like to be your friend. This time when you fill out the chart, you are talking about YOUR actions and how they may have made the other person feel.

For example:

Person's name or initials: _____ **MY SISTER** _____

What happened?	When did it happen?	How do you think they felt?
I told my little sister we could hang out later but then when she came by my bedroom I shouted, "get out loser!"	Monday	Rejected

Your turn. Reflect back on the past week. How might your actions have affected someone else either positively or negatively?

Person's name or initials: _____

What happened?	When did it happen?	How do you think they felt?

After looking at the interactions, do you see a pattern? Do you think you were manipulating, abusing, or grooming this person, even unintentionally? Why?

Do you need to make changes to your relationships? What might be causing you to treat this person in this manner?

It can be hard to honestly and critically examine our own actions this way, but it's a crucial step in developing healthy relationships. In the end, it benefits everyone!

TO SUM UP

- Developing self-worth when you are in a complicated relationship can be very difficult.
- Just because someone you trust and care about normalizes something, doesn't make it safe, healthy, or right for you.
- Grooming is a severe case of manipulation that can lead a person to do things they wouldn't normally do in order to stay in the good graces of someone they care about. Relationships should be built on mutual respect and trust, not manipulation, coercion, or fear.

SECTION 5

HOW DO WE GET IT?

Wouldn't it be great if we could just say, "Wear this shirt, like this music, say these words, and poof—you will be likable!" Well, we can't say that, and that's probably a good thing, because if everyone was likable in the same way, it would be really boring. While there are general tips to be likable and avoid being unlikable, it's also really important for people to keep the parts of themselves that make them unique. And that means there's probably a distinct way for every single person to be more likable—by being a likable version of who they are. Think about who you really are deep down inside, and make only small adjustments to avoid the pitfalls that make people unlikable.

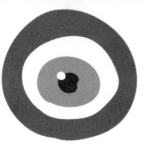

Chapter 12

How to Be Likable

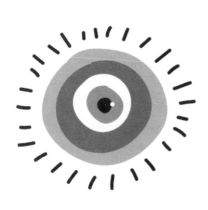

There's not just one way to be likable! Because we're all unique, and all our situations are different, people's preferences, interests, and experiences are all a part of being the most likable you. Understanding how you are interpreting social cues around you and whether you have realistic expectations for your relationships is also part of it. These are important steps towards greater likability because we have to be adaptable to new situations where we want to fit in, and we have to make sure our past experiences don't overly influence us to act in ways that may not apply to the people we want to hang out with today.

Let's think about ways we can improve our likability. Remember that likable people make others feel happy, valued, and/or included. There are many ways to achieve that, but what works in one situation may not work in another. So here we want to talk about paying attention to social norms—in other words, what seems common and accepted when around others.

Rank Likable Traits

Make a list of some traits that you think make someone likable, in order from most important to least important. How are you similar or different to the traits you described?

Traits	Do you have these traits?
1.	
2.	
3.	
4.	
5.	

Have you ever noticed that likable people tend to be leaders that others look up to? Not because they are "cool" necessarily, but because people trust them and feel like it is safe to follow their lead. Likable people often gain that trust by spending a lot of time asking questions, listening, and focusing on how a group works before they interact within it. Research has shown that people are much more likely to become great friends when their first interactions included many, many questions of each other—kind of a way to find common ground in interests, and a way of feeling closer to one another. That makes sense, right? A person who talks about themselves a lot or tries to show off when we first meet them is usually not someone we like a lot. But a person who wants to get to know us usually makes us feel good, or valued, or important.

Likable people don't only ask questions, however. They also contribute to conversations in ways that show that they understand others and are tuning into the general feeling or the vibe of the group. If everyone is laughing, they tell a joke that is kind of like the jokes others are telling (just as corny, or risky, or sarcastic as the group seems to like). If people are generating new ideas, likable people do, too, but defer to others to show that they heard what others said too, and respect all ideas. It's not about being a "copycat," it's more like a rally in ping pong where you are trying to keep the ball on the table as long as possible. That means you have to match your opponent in strength and direction. You are not trying to overpower the person, you are trying to engage them in order to play as long as possible. Likable people do this in conversation. By understanding the direction of the group and adding to the conversation to keep it moving in a similar direction, everyone feels validated and included. Let's give it a try:

Likable Ping Pong

How do you keep the conversation going? Read the examples in the box on the left, and then circle the response that you think would make someone more likable.

What They Said	Circle the Better Response
Someone tells a joke about a chicken crossing the road.	1. You tell the dirtiest joke you know 2. You tell a similar joke but about a cow
Someone starts talking about their favorite band.	3. You ask more about the genre of music and share the name of your favorite band 4. You brag about the time you met the lead singer of a different band
Someone talks about the new Netflix show they just started.	5. You talk about the party you are going to this weekend 6. You talk about what you are watching and/or reading

Correct Answers: 2, 3 & 6 - These answers keep the conversation going.

So next time you're in a group setting, stop and pay attention to the group dynamic. Even if it's your current group of friends, where you already fit in—take a moment to observe the group as if you were an outsider. How would the group dynamic seem? What could someone do that would make them seem to fit in right away? What would make them seem like even more of an outsider? Practicing thinking about these things in comfortable situations can help prepare you for the next time you're the new person.

Likable people are also more likely than others to maintain nice eye contact when first meeting someone, or smile more frequently (if it is a situation when smiling would make sense—not at a funeral, for instance), and also are more likely to have an open posture with their body language (for example, they have their arms to their sides, not folded in front of them). These subtle signals are remarkably powerful.

Some research has shown that people form impressions of one another even before they speak, and when people seem mopey or closed off, it actually makes other people observing them feel sad. But when people seem more open and pleasant, it gives observers a mood boost, and eventually people recognize that they always tend to feel good when they are around that open-postured person (in other words, that person becomes likable!).

Research suggests that once likable people seem to understand what's normal in a group, and act in ways that seem similar to how the group behaves, they tend to start interacting a little more than others. When they do, it is with confidence (not as an obvious way to try and become more likable). It's not necessarily important to be extroverted to be likable—shy people are highly likable too! What's more important is that when speaking, likable people are genuinely interested in being kind, fair, equitable, and doing what's best for the group, rather than being self-focused. What we discussed earlier about self-esteem, self-worth, and peer-esteem is a big part of this!

TO SUM UP

- Asking questions and listening to answers is a great way to find common ground and build relationships.
- Contributing to a conversation is different than dominating a conversation. Likable people tend to ask more questions that promote conversation rather than just talking about themselves endlessly.
- Likable people are genuinely interested in being kind, fair, equitable, and doing what's best for the group, rather than being self-focused.
- We can learn a lot about our current relationships by paying attention to the group dynamic.
- Now that you know what makes someone likable, you can begin to shift your own behaviors to have a more positive outcome.

CHAPTER 13

EMOTIONAL INTELLIGENCE

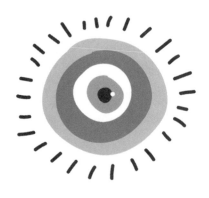

Psychologists have identified an area of our intelligence that is especially important for our future happiness and success. It's called Emotional Intelligence (EI), which is all about how well we read others' feelings, understand subtle differences between them, and change our behavior in response. People with high emotional intelligence not only understand how they feel and why, but they also understand how their actions affect how others feel. Very likable people have high emotional intelligence. And, interestingly, these abilities can change; they can get better (or worse). You can learn how to be a more emotionally intelligent human!

Let's start by getting a baseline of your EI and then think about areas that may warrant improvement and how you can do that. This quiz will look at each area, and you will be able to score it yourself.

EI and Likability

Read the following statements[2] about your emotions and feelings and indicate your level of agreement or disagreement.

I often pay attention to my feelings	Not like me	Somewhat like me	Totally ME!
I am rarely confused about how I feel	Not like me	Somewhat like me	Totally ME!
I usually care about what I am feeling	Not like me	Somewhat like me	Totally ME!
No matter how badly I feel, I try to think about pleasant things	Not like me	Somewhat like me	Totally ME!
I am usually very clear about my feelings	Not like me	Somewhat like me	Totally ME!
Although I am sometimes sad, I have a mostly optimistic outlook	Not like me	Somewhat like me	Totally ME!

2   Items adapted from Salovey, P., Mayer, J. D., Goldman, S. L., Turvey, C., & Palfai, T. P. (1995). Emotional attention, clarity, and repair: Exploring emotional intelligence using the Trait Meta-Mood Scale. In J. W. Pennebaker (Ed), *Emotion, disclosure, and health.* (pp. 125–154). American Psychological Association. https://doi-org. libproxy.lib.unc.edu/10.1037/10182-006

These questions each tap into different markers of emotional intelligence. Remember, emotional intelligence is not just about understanding how you feel. It is about knowing how to change your feelings when you want to. Easier said than done though, right?

Well, changing it might be easier than you think! A lot of learning to increase your emotional intelligence comes from just learning to stop and pay attention to your emotions. Once you start paying attention, actually changing the feeling can be surprisingly doable. Some people can change how they feel by thinking about where their feelings come from and recognizing when they may be overreacting or jumping to conclusions. Other people can change their feelings by thinking about the future and realizing that they are brooding over something that won't be so bad in a week or month or year, or by thinking about how strong they have been in the past when dealing with tough situations. Some people can distract themselves by doing something fun and then later realize that it was an effective way to make themselves feel better. Still others feel better when they talk with someone they trust to get their advice or to feel validated.

One thing that rarely works, however, is when people simply try to avoid their feelings and pretend they will just go away.

Are there times when you avoid your feelings? If so, what are some safe ways that you can discuss them, confront then, or think about them more often?

Everyone is different.

What are three ways that help you feel better most effectively when you are feeling upset, lonely, or worried? Believe it or not, just knowing to stop and do these things is a big part of emotional intelligence!

What are some behaviors you can engage in when you are feeling most stressed? These might be some calming, enjoyable activities like you probably had for the last question, or they could be activities that help you plan and deal with whatever is stressing you out.

Emotional intelligence is one way of thinking about how you can best get along with others and be likable. Understanding your own emotions, emotional reactions, and how others feel is an important way to be connected with people in a real way. The more authentic you are with others, and the more genuine they are with you, the closer you will be.

TO SUM UP

- Emotional intelligence refers to how well we understand and can change our feelings, or how well we understand the feelings of others.
- We can improve our emotional intelligence with practice.
- The more we think about how to regulate our own feelings, the better we understand ourselves and the feelings of those around us.

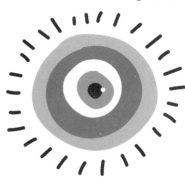

Chapter 14

AVOIDING TEMPTATION TO SEEK STATUS

Wanting popularity based on status is so common in middle and high school because the status-popular kids seem to have it all. But there is a price to status that can often be more costly than you would have imagined.

It's not uncommon to hear stories of people who tear down those around them to try and keep a hold of their power. They allow the desire for control to override their need to connect. This is often the reason why status-seekers are at a greater risk of depression, anxiety, and trouble with addictions as compared to less-popular people. Status-seekers

Charlee was a HOTT GIRL. This was the name the group gave to themselves: according to this group, they were so hot, they needed an extra "T" in their title. But other groups who were not so enamored with their self-proclamations (or maybe were envious of their status) called them THOT. Regardless, HOTT was popular! Adults were charmed by them, and classmates wanted to be a part of the group. When they walked the halls, it was as if they walked in slow motion with a wind machine blowing their hair in just the right way. They were beautiful, popular... AND they had a mean streak.

One afternoon Charlee posted a TikTok and then refreshed the app about a million times waiting for the likes and comments to roll in. It was silent! Charlee spent most of the night obsessing over why her video wasn't getting the attention it deserved.

The next day at school, her "friends" were telling inside jokes and giggling about something that Charlee didn't understand. "What the heck!" she lashed out. "Why are you guys ignoring me?"

The HOTT GIRLS didn't respond with words but their body language told the whole story. Charlee was OUT!

As soon as she got home she went on TikTok to find hundreds of comments about her being ugly and fat and that no one at the school would ever hook up with her. Within moments, Charlee went from being at the top of the food chain to being the chum.

As Charlee cried that night and thought about how she would enact her revenge, two other thoughts kept creeping into her mind... that she had done the exact same thing to Sydney a few months before, and that it's so hard to stay on top.

tend to have trouble with relationships when they are in their 20s, 30s, and 40s. As adults, their friends and significant others say that they seem "stuck-up," too focused still on status, and use people rather than actually be supportive or interested in others. There's even research to suggest that those who are very high in status as teens are more likely than others to get fired or demoted as adults.

But trying not to focus on status is easier said than done! We know. So let's try a few things and see if it helps move you away from seeking status and towards seeking likability. It starts with recognizing intentions (what you hope to accomplish, such as garnering attention) and triggers (the feeling or moment that prompted you to act).

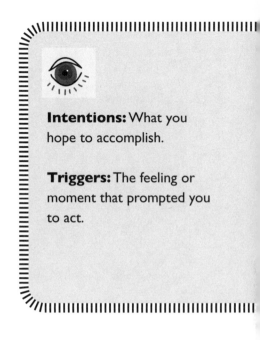

Intentions: What you hope to accomplish.

Triggers: The feeling or moment that prompted you to act.

Observation of a Status-Seeker

How do you define a status-seeker? What traits or actions do you associate with this label? Create a list of behaviors you associate with status-seekers, and think about times you may have seen examples of these traits in real life. What were the outcomes of those actions?

Behaviors	Real-life examples	Outcomes

Intentions and Triggers

YES   NO   When you spend time with a particular group, are you more consumed with status-seeking?

YES   NO   Do you mindlessly scroll through your social media feed feeling unworthy or jealous?

YES   NO   Are you constantly checking texts, comments, and stories out of a fear of missing out (FOMO)?

These are some common triggers for people, so don't feel bad if you answered yes to some or all of them. This just lets you know that paying attention to these triggers, and to your intentions in social spaces, will be a helpful step.

If you answered "yes" to any of these questions, you may be feeling that your behaviors or habits are worth changing if the end result means more confidence, higher self-esteem, stronger and deeper relationships, and knowing you are becoming likable. Let's try something that may feel a bit dramatic at first but can yield amazing results!

Take a Break

For one week turn off, deactivate, or block accounts that trigger a negative response (feeling unworthy, jealous, FOMO, etc.). In the table on the next pages, track how you feel about certain situations. We've listed a few examples you can use, but go ahead and fill in some that are more specific to you, too. Measure how you feel at the beginning of the week and then come back to the activity at the end of the week and complete the last column. For this activity to work you really need to commit to not looking (not even a sneak peek over a friend's shoulder!). Add the number corresponding with the feeling.

1 = Strong Disagree	2 = Disagree	3 = Neutral	4 = Agree	5 = Strongly Agree

Statement	At the start of the week	At the end of the week
When I go on vacation, I continue to keep tabs on what my friends are doing via social media.		
I feel bothered/concerned when I don't collect many likes, views, or subscribers after posting a picture or video.		
When I can't be near my phone (or any other device) for a while, I wonder what's being discussed or what's trending that I am missing.		

FOMO and Decision-Making

Let's look at the role of FOMO—one of the biggest triggers for lots of people!—in some of your decision-making. Write about an incident where FOMO played a major role in your actions. Did you reach out to someone directly? Did you cry alone in your room? Did you say, "It doesn't bother me" when really you still felt hurt? Did you sneak out of the house to participate in something even though you knew there would be major consequences to pay?

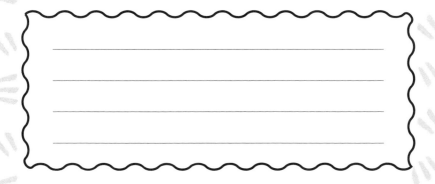

In order to avoid the trap of status-seeking, it is important to identify our intentions. Do they really serve our best interest, or are we reacting to a trigger? When we fall prey to triggers we tend to focus on control rather than connection, and often end up making decisions that cause pain (to others and to ourselves). In the earlier example, Charlee was so concerned with being left out (the trigger), that her main focus was to try to rise back up the social chain. A more helpful response would've been to take a hard look at her current relationships and her past behavior and decide what kind of person she wanted to be moving forward.

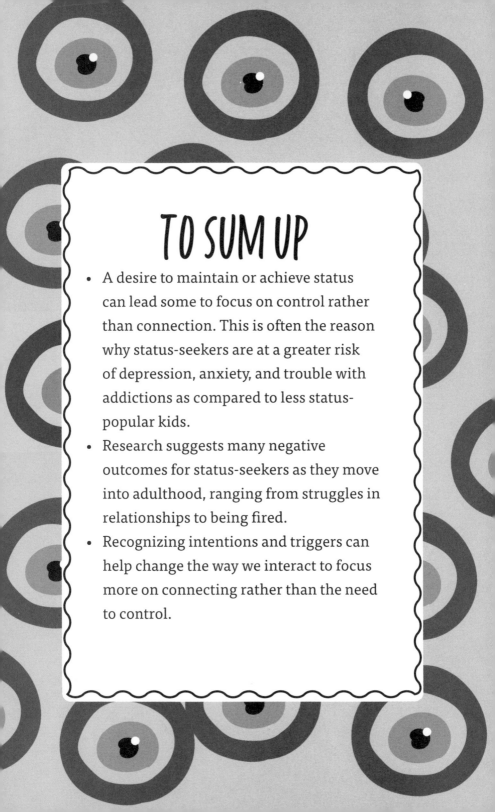

TO SUM UP

- A desire to maintain or achieve status can lead some to focus on control rather than connection. This is often the reason why status-seekers are at a greater risk of depression, anxiety, and trouble with addictions as compared to less status-popular kids.
- Research suggests many negative outcomes for status-seekers as they move into adulthood, ranging from struggles in relationships to being fired.
- Recognizing intentions and triggers can help change the way we interact to focus more on connecting rather than the need to control.

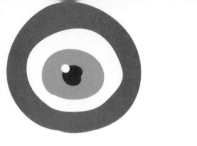

CHAPTER 15

MAKING A PLAN

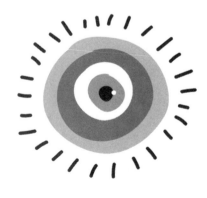

As we start making changes to our behavior, sometimes anxiety can get in the way. Big feelings about a situation or a change can make us think that a feeling will last forever, when in fact, it is just a sensation in the moment. Think of these big feelings like clouds in the sky: they can be bright or dark, big or small, heavy or light. However, regardless of their color, shape, and size, they will eventually move on and disappear. When we think about our desire to change our behavior, to build new and better relationships, or to be true to who we really want to be, those big feelings can sometimes cloud our judgment. They can make us create a narrative that fits those big feelings but may not be in our best interest as we move forward. Setting goals is one way we can learn to look past those big feelings.

Setting goals to work on your likability (rather than status) acts as a road map to developing more self-confidence and building better relationships. Every time your mind starts to trick you into believing that you're stuck in one place and can't move forward, look at your goals. You can always move forward: but in order to do that, it is important to set goals that are realistic enough that you can stick with them. So we'll work on setting small goals that can build on each other. It's easy to stick with something when you truly believe the outcome is worth it! Writing these goals down gives you something to look at, and reminds you why you are doing what you are doing and that your path (your small goals) over time will lead you to your destination.

Setting Goals

Use the map to plan your journey. Go back to the beginning of this section and Chapter 12. Review your observations regarding how you are similar and different to those you deem likable. Think about where you are starting (how you are feeling about your own popularity today), what is your destination (identify what type of popularity will yield the greatest benefits to you) and how you will get there (what realistic goals you can set to achieve the desired outcome). When setting small goals, focus on actions you can do today and in the moment.

For example:

START: I worry constantly about what others think of me.

FINISH: I want to have a great group of friends where I feel accepted and appreciated.

GOAL 1: Exercise each day (so I feel good about myself).

GOAL 2: Take a break from social media (so I stop comparing myself to everyone else and feeling left out).

GOAL 3: Spend more time with person X (who is kind and we have fun together) and less time with person Y (who always makes me doubt myself and the things I say).

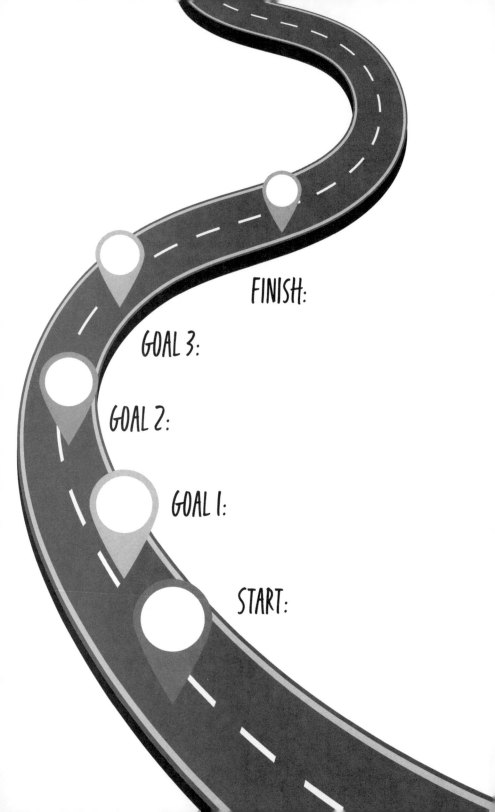

FINISH:

GOAL 3:

GOAL 2:

GOAL 1:

START:

Logging Changes: What did you do differently today?

Come back to your road map in a week. Did you attempt to meet a small goal? What did you do? How did it work? How did others respond?

What's the next step? If you didn't achieve your goal, think about how your actions made you (or others) feel. Do you have some ideas for how you can adjust your actions or expectations to try again? If it did work, great! What's your next small goal?

Self-Care Check-In

As you begin to make specific changes, you will need to check in on how you are feeling. Are you anxious, worried, scared, frustrated, or sad? Write about a specific situation (regarding your road map) and describe how the actions you took to meet your goal made you feel.

Remember, big feelings are normal even if they are not what you want them to be. When writing down those feelings, try to remember the cloud analogy. Can you watch those big feelings from a distance the way you watch a cloud drift through the sky? Rather than being IN the big feeling, try writing about it objectively as if you are watching it happen from afar.

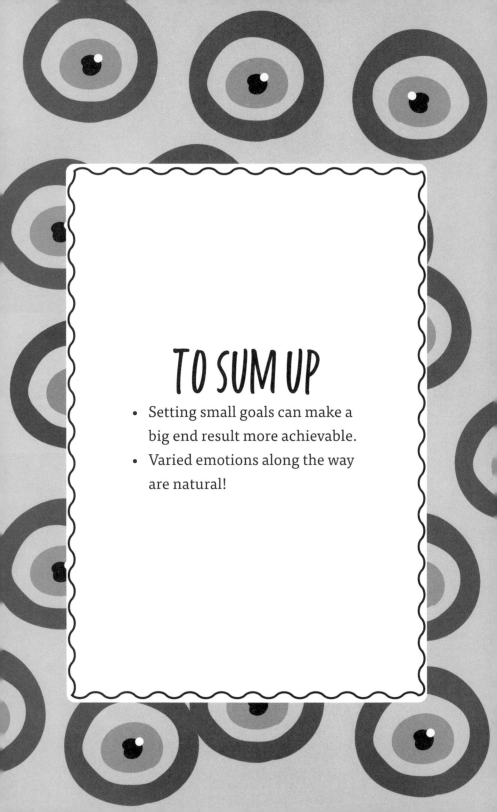

TO SUM UP

- Setting small goals can make a big end result more achievable.
- Varied emotions along the way are natural!

Chapter 16

MANAGING EXPECTATIONS

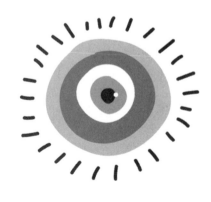

We all have those moments where we try something and hope (or expect) to be great at it without putting in the time and effort it takes to get it right. Managing expectations is about practice and patience, and when it comes to navigating the right kind of popularity, too often our need to achieve the desired outcome gets the better of our stamina. We know, logically, that it takes time and effort... but it can be hard to remember that in the moment!

Think about a basketball player—Lebron James, for example. Becoming one of the world's greatest basketball players didn't happen overnight and didn't happen just because he learned the plays and practiced shooting. Lebron James often talks about what it is to be a champion. It is everything from his dedication to his physical practice to his deep understanding of the importance of mindset. His road map consists of small and big goals, everything from running and lifting weights and practicing shots to meditation and mindfulness. His road map even accounts for wind that may blow him off course temporarily and how he plans to get back on the highway. He is successful because he understands that being a champion on the court and in life is a mindset that affects each and every decision he makes. His road map is not a quick or straight line to reaching the end goal. So like Lebron, make sure to manage your expectations; if you do, you'll be less likely to be derailed by setbacks or things not happening fast enough.

Sometimes we try something only to be disappointed by the outcome. Maybe we put ourselves out there and try to sit with a new group at lunch, or compliment someone we don't know well, only to receive glares and confused looks. That's why managing expectations is so important. Lebron doesn't throw in the towel after a bad game, he looks at what didn't work, makes the necessary changes, and goes right back out the next game with his campion mindset still in place. Change takes time, change takes trial and error. Change takes managing expectations. Take a moment to reflect on your own feelings about how slowly or quickly things are progressing. Be honest with yourself about what you want and then be realistic about how you can continue to achieve progress.

_____

_____

_____

_____

_____

_____

_____

_____

_____

_____

_____

_____

_____

_____

_____

_____

Setbacks often lead us to learn the most. And the more complicated the change we are trying to achieve, the more setbacks we can expect to occur. The best way to deal with these is to think about how you will handle setbacks before they happen.

What will you do if something embarrassing happens or you feel rejected? What will you say out loud and what will you tell yourself?

What are some of the fears or worries you may have while trying to take these steps?

What are some of the things you learned from this workbook, or elsewhere, that you can remind yourself of if you experience those fears?

What are some other barriers that would keep you from being able to take these three steps?

What is your plan to overcome these barriers?

_____

_____

_____

_____

_____

_____

_____

_____

_____

_____

_____

_____

_____

_____

_____

TO SUM UP

- All feelings pass, no matter how overwhelming they seem in the moment.
- Change takes time and patience; everyone faces setbacks.
- Having a plan to deal with setbacks and big emotions will help you cope with them and keep moving forward when the time comes.

CONCLUSION

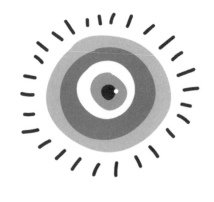

Popularity is something we begin talking about in elementary school and continue to discuss through adulthood. For certain people, being popular is a badge of honor, for some it something to aspire to, and for others, it's complicated. Whatever your relationship with popularity has been in the past, we hope this workbook has helped you understand the difference between status and likability. Being human is dynamic: we get to change and grow and learn. We get to reflect on past experiences using newly acquired vocabulary and understanding and choose to make the changes to better ourselves. So we want to say, congratulations! By completing this workbook you now understand the science behind popularity, the different types of popularity, and the importance of finding and becoming the right kind of popular. Hopefully, along this journey you have learned a little about yourself and who you want to be. We hope that this workbook is something you will come back to as you grow and be able to look back and see just how far you've come.

GLOSSARY

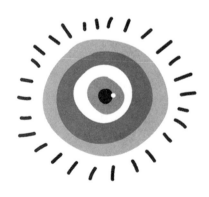

Accepted (on the likability matrix): people that are generally well-liked and well-thought of by most other people

Attention-seeking: Doing something to keep all eyes on you

Average (on the likability matrix): people who have solid social connections, but aren't necessarily well-known or high in status

Bias: the way we tend to interpret the world and things that happen around us

Confidence: the knowledge that you and the things you do are relevant and even important

Controversial (on the likability matrix): people who tend to either be very liked or very disliked; few others have neutral feelings about them

Cue interpretations: the idea that we all have a different way of interpreting what we see and hear

Dopamine: a neurochemical responsible for good feelings

Emotional Intelligence (EI): how well we read others' feelings, understand subtle differences between them, and change our behavior in response

Fame: Being known or talked about by many

Floaters (in social groups): those who don't have a set position as they tend to move from group to group with ease

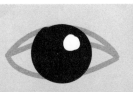

Followers (in social groups): those happy to go along

FOMO: Fear of missing out

Fringe (in social groups): not having a central part of the group, being more on the periphery

Grooming: a process by which an individual normalizes certain topics or behaviors in order to gain the trust and loyalty of another person

Influencer: Someone well-known enough that they can "influence" trends; often paid to spread information about popular products and events

Intentions: What you hope to accomplish

Leaders (in social groups): those in charge

Likability (in popularity): the type of acceptance based on true connections

Likability matrix: a graph describing the levels of likability

Neglected (on the likability matrix): those who are not generally thought of in social situations, but not actively excluded

Oxytocin: a neurotransmitter that helps us form social connections

Peer-esteem: the regard in which another person holds an individual

Popularity: from "for the people"; a word used to indicate someone's acceptance, that can have meanings referring to both status and likability

Prefrontal cortex: the "thinking" part of the brain, which keeps us from acting impulsively; the brain's "brakes"

Rejected (on the likability matrix): those who are regularly actively shunned from social connections

Self-esteem: having respect for yourself or a positive impression of yourself

Self-worth: the belief that you are worthy of respect and consideration

Social norms: what seems common and accepted when around others

Social rewards: the good feeling people get when they think others are admiring, imitating, agreeing with, or even just looking at them

Status (in popularity): the type of acceptance focused on power

Triggers: the feeling or moment that prompted you to act

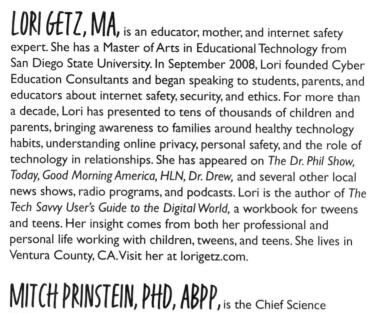

LORI GETZ, MA, is an educator, mother, and internet safety

expert. She has a Master of Arts in Educational Technology from San Diego State University. In September 2008, Lori founded Cyber Education Consultants and began speaking to students, parents, and educators about internet safety, security, and ethics. For more than a decade, Lori has presented to tens of thousands of children and parents, bringing awareness to families around healthy technology habits, understanding online privacy, personal safety, and the role of technology in relationships. She has appeared on *The Dr. Phil Show, Today, Good Morning America, HLN, Dr. Drew,* and several other local news shows, radio programs, and podcasts. Lori is the author of *The Tech Savvy User's Guide to the Digital World,* a workbook for tweens and teens. Her insight comes from both her professional and personal life working with children, tweens, and teens. She lives in Ventura County, CA. Visit her at lorigetz.com.

MITCH PRINSTEIN, PHD, ABPP, is the Chief Science

Officer of the American Psychological Association and the John Van Seters Distinguished Professor of Psychology and Neuroscience at the University of North Carolina at Chapel Hill. For over 25 years, Mitch's research has examined adolescent peer relationships, leading to over 150 peer-reviewed papers and nine books, including *Popular: Finding Happiness and Success in a World That Cares Too Much About the Wrong Kinds of Relationships.* Mitch's work has been featured in over 200 pieces in *The New York Times, The Wall Street Journal,* National Public Radio, *The Los Angeles Times,* CNN, *U.S. News & World Report, Time* magazine, *New York* magazine, *Newsweek, Reuters, Family Circle, Real Simple, All Things Considered,* and two TEDx talks. Visit him @mitchprinstein on twitter.

MAGINATION PRESS is the children's book imprint of the

American Psychological Association. APA works to advance psychology as a science and profession and as a means of promoting health and human welfare. Magination Press books reach young readers and their parents and caregivers to make navigating life's challenges a little easier. It's the combined power of psychology and literature that makes a Magination Press book special. Visit maginationpress.org and @MaginationPress on Facebook, Twitter, Instagram, and Pinterest.